BAD ALICE

Jean Ure

BAD ALICE

Jean Ure

Hodder
Children's
Books

A division of Hodder Headline Limited

*With thanks to John Simmonds at the
British Association for Adoption and Fostering
for his work as a consultant on this novel.*

First published in paperback in Great Britain in 2003
by Hodder Children's Books

A catalogue record for this book is available
from the British Library

ISBN 0 340 81760 7

Typeset in NewBaskerville by Avon DataSet Ltd,
Bidford-on-Avon, Warwickshire

Printed and bound in Great Britain by
Bookmarque Ltd., Croydon, Surrey

The paper and board used in this paperback by
Hodder Children's Books are natural recyclable products
made from wood grown in sustainable forests.
The manufacturing processes conform to the environmental
regulations of the country of origin.

Hodder Children's Books
a Division of Hodder Headline Limited
338 Euston Road
London NW1 3BH

For Leonard, with love.

1

This is the story of last summer. The summer I stayed with my nan, while Mum took Charlotte to America. The summer I met Alice . . .

Bold, bad Alice! Alice, who told lies. Who was aggressive; anti-social; couldn't be trusted. Just about no one had a good word to say for bad Alice.

It was Steven who first told me about her. Steven was Nan's desperate attempt to find me a friend for all the long hot months I was going to be staying with her. His mum and dad were members of Nan's church. I don't go to church myself, it's something I never even think about, but Nan goes all the time. She got what Mum calls 'the bug' a few years back, when she went to hear some preacher guy from California, and got hooked. She takes it very seriously. She's not holy, or anything; she doesn't go on about it. Like, she wouldn't ever try to convert me to her way of thinking. But I know that it means a lot to her so even though I don't share her beliefs I do my best to respect her feelings. It seems only fair.

Anyway, she'd gone and invited these people over for tea, Sunday afternoon.

'They'll be bringing Steven with them. He's such a nice lad! And just about your age. Twelve. That's not too young, is it? I suppose thirteen's not too grand to talk to twelve?'

I pictured Steven as being very clean and scrubbed. Very earnest. Very shining and polite. This is my prejudice showing through. Like all people who go to church have haloes round them. And are good. OK! *Geeky*. I'll admit it. I make determined efforts not to be prejudiced, but sometimes you just can't seem to help it. And in this case I was well wrong, since Steven was just the kind of tough nut we have a lot of in my school and whom I spend my entire life trying to avoid.

I couldn't avoid Steven 'cos the whole point of him being there was that we should be pushed off together.

'Why don't you two boys go into the garden?' said Nan, all bright and beaming. 'I'll call you when tea's ready. Go on! Off you go.' And she opened the back door and shooed us out like we were a couple of little diddy kids from Reception. 'Duffy,' she said, 'show Steven the fox earth. He'd like to see that. We've got our very own fox,' she said to Steven.

Nan kills me sometimes. I mean, she's really great, and I love her to bits, but she just has *no idea*. Steven stood there, his face wooden, his expression a complete blank. He didn't have the least interest in going to see a fox earth. You could tell. He'd far rather be out with his mates, kicking a football.

'Duffy's seen the fox, haven't you?' said Nan.

2

I nodded, trying not to squirm. Steven gave me this look of utter contempt. Nan, oblivious, sent us on our way with a little push.

Off you go, kiddies! Go play in the sandpit.

I stumbled out, over the back doorstep. Steven followed, more slowly, like an automaton. He seemed a bit dazed. Probably still trying to figure out what he was doing here. I could sort of sympathize. I could see that a sunny Sunday afternoon stuck with a dim nerd like me would hardly be anyone's idea of fun.

Nan was still smiling. Determinedly taking no notice. She was the one who had set it up, of course; her and Steven's mum.

'I've got my grandson staying with me for the summer ... it would be so nice if he and Steven could get to know each other!'

To a grown-up, I guess, it would make perfect sense. We were both boys, weren't we? What could be more natural? Get together! Be friends!

'I'll stay here and get the tea,' beamed Nan.

She closed the door and I felt this familiar sinking sensation in the pit of my stomach. Now there was no help for it, I was on my own – and it was up to me to do the entertaining. After all, it was my nan's garden.

I opened my mouth to say something. Start the entertaining.

'F-f-fox – fox – fff–'

No use. It wasn't going to happen; the words weren't going to come.

'D-d-dow – dow—'

Down there. You'd think it would be simple enough. But nothing's ever simple, with me. I flapped a hand and set off towards the fox earth, Steven slouching at my side.

It's only a smallish sort of garden, is Nan's, but even a smallish garden is better than no garden at all. We don't have one at home; not any more. Not now we live in a flat. Nan's garden is mostly grass and flowerbeds, with a crumbly brick wall at the end behind a tangle of brambles. Under the brambles is where the fox earth was.

I pointed. 'F-f-fox earth.'

I stood back, for Steven to see. Not that he was interested.

'Yeah.' He barely even glanced. He seemed more concerned with looking over the wall into the garden on the other side. 'Lots of 'em round here. They're vermin, foxes are.'

I said, 'Who s-says?'

'My mum,' said Steven. 'They raid the dustbins. Make a right mess.'

'Our one doesn't,' I said. 'We leave f-food out for her.'

'Didn't ought to do that,' said Steven. 'Only encourages 'em. They eat people's cats.'

I resented that. I happen to be one of those people who believe the fox is much maligned.

'F-foxes don't eat c-*cats*,' I said.

'My mum says they do. Says they eat babies, an' all.'

I couldn't help thinking that Steven's mother must be

4

an extremely ignorant person, but I didn't like to say so. I mean, for one thing this boy was a guest, in my garden, and it would have seemed pretty rude; for another, I wasn't sure I could get the words out. Not without a lot of munching and chewing, which would just embarrass the both of us. So I shut up, while Steven trampled through the undergrowth and went to peer over the wall.

'Weirdo lives there,' he said. 'Alice Gregory. Goes to my school. She's a basket case.'

My first introduction to Alice. A basket case.

'Her dad goes to our church. Knows your gran. Knows my mum and dad. He's all right. He's great! But that Alice, she's a total nutter. Has these mad fits.'

'Like h-how?' I said.

'Like she'll suddenly attack people. For absolutely no reason. Got sent home last term. Attacked this girl, Rosie Nolan? Put her hands round her throat and yelled that she was going to kill her. Way out, man! Took six teachers to drag her off. Well, two, at any rate. My mum says she oughtn't to be allowed in school with normal people. Says she's a danger.'

I thought, *oh yeah?* I didn't actually say it (for reasons mentioned above) but I really wasn't sure that Steven's mum knew what she was talking about. She'd said foxes ate babies. I personally wouldn't place too much importance on the opinion of anyone who said a thing like that.

'Sooner you than me,' said Steven. 'Living with mad Alice at the end of the garden . . . never know what she might get up to. Might come flying over and throttle you!'

'I expect it'll be all right,' I said.

'That's what you think! I reckon she ought to be locked up. Not normal, the way she carries on. If she's not going berserk, attacking people, she's, like, refusing to talk. Won't say a word for days on end, sometimes. Completely *doo*lally.' He put a finger to his head and twisted it. 'Raving nut case.'

A silence fell over us. The thought occurred to me that not speaking for days on end might not be so bad. It might even be a relief. Not having to worry all the time about how the words were going to come out – or even *whether* they were going to come out. Not having to see the expressions on people's faces. 'Poor boy! Such a shame!' 'So sad! Obviously brain damaged.'

'So where d'you live, then?' said Steven. 'Normally?'

I concentrated, very hard, on digging a little pit in the sandy soil of the fox earth with the toe of my trainer. Sometimes it helps. A kind of . . . displacement activity.

'B-B-Bushey.'

'Where's that?'

'N-near W-Watford.'

'Other side o' London?'

'Yeah.'

Steven bent and picked up a stone.

'So what's it like, in Watford?'

As if he cared. He was just trying to make conversation.

It should have been me who was making conversation! I opened my mouth and tried to arrange some words. The least I could do was respond to questions.

'It's not much d-different from P-P-P—'

Purley. But it wouldn't come.

'FROM HERE!' I yelled.

I didn't mean to yell. It just sometimes happens that way. It's like there's this blockage, then everything suddenly bursts out at full volume.

Nan would have warned Steven's mum. They always warn people. She would have told her, for sure. And Steven's mum would have told Steven. 'He's got something wrong with him. He talks funny.'

She must have told him! Even so, he had one of those looks on his face. An *I don't know which way to look* sort of look.

'Here all summer?' he said.

I would have liked to say, 'Yeah, but it's OK, we don't have to see each other. I don't want to, any more than you do.' Instead, I jerked my head (an involuntary action) and went 'Mm!'.

I was here all summer. Week after week, after long, long week.

'So which football team d'you support?'

Poor guy! He was really trying. He wasn't to know I'm the only bloke in the entire Western hemisphere who doesn't follow football. But you can't admit to it; not when they already think you're two slices short of a sandwich. So I said what I always say.

Tried to say what I always say.

'W–W–'

Start again.

'W–W–'

Take a deep breath. That sometimes solves the problem.

'W–W–'

And then again, it sometimes doesn't.

'W-WATFORD!' I bawled.

You could practically see the decibels, thudding round the garden. Steven looked a bit alarmed; perhaps he hadn't been warned about the shouting. He flung his stone over the wall and picked up another one. I went into my twitching routine. It's this thing I do when I get stressed.

Steven, very pointedly, looked the other way. I went on twitching. This wasn't working! I felt really mad at Nan for pushing me into it. I knew she meant well, she just wanted to find me a friend for the summer, but the truth is I can't make friends the same as other people. I'm too much of a liability. I embarrass them. Like I'd embarrassed Dad, so that in the end he couldn't take any more of it and left home. You'd have thought Nan would realize by now!

I headed back, abruptly, up the garden.

'Go see 'f tea's ready!'

It wasn't; but at least there was safety in numbers. The rest of them could talk, and I could just contribute the occasional grunt. It's easier that way.

Later, when we were on our own, Nan said, 'Well! How did you get on?'

I hunched a shoulder. 'OK.'

'Going to see each other again?' Nan waited, hopefully. 'Made any arrangements?'

'Mm-hm.' I shook my head.

'No?'

I knew she was disappointed. The thing is, Nan works every morning, nine o'clock till one; and what was I going to do with myself all those long hours while she was out? I'd tried to reassure her.

'I'll be all right!'

I'm used to being on my own; I'm happy on my own. But she just couldn't believe me. She's a very sociable kind of person, my nan. She belongs to all these clubs, she has nights out with the girls (elderly women, just like Nan), she goes to church every Sunday and does lots of churchy things. Fetes and fairs and jumble sales. She just can never understand how someone can be happy with only themselves for company.

'You're going to be so bored!'

I told her that I wouldn't be. 'I've got the computer.'

'Computer!' Nan holds the computer in deepest scorn. Privately I reckon she's a bit scared of it. She'd gone out and bought one so that she could move with the times, but until that summer when I went to stay she had barely even looked at it. 'Computer's no way of life,' she said.

It was, I thought, if you couldn't make friends.

'Horrible thing! Sitting there staring at you.'

She does make me laugh at times. 'Nan,' I said, 'it's fun!'

'Might be, if you could make any sense of it,' said Nan.

'I could always teach you. It's really easy . . . even babies can learn.'

'All right. You're on!' Nan jumped to her feet. She's still pretty spry, in spite of her age. 'Put your money where your mouth is . . . come and show me!'

'We could go and e-mail Mum,' I said.

'Good idea! What shall we say? We're doing OK? Tell her she's not to worry?'

'Yeah.' I nodded. I knew I couldn't tell Mum that I was missing her, and missing Charlotte, and even, sometimes, still missing Dad. Mum had enough to cope with. All I had to do was get through the summer.

'Well, come on, then,' said Nan. 'Stir your stumps. No time like the present!'

2

'I'll be off, now, then,' said Nan. 'Duffy?' She put her head round the bedroom door. 'I said, *I'm off!*'

Underneath the duvet, I made a mumbling sound. I was still half asleep and couldn't get my mouth going.

'You're sure you'll be all right, by yourself?'

'Mm.' I managed a grunt and moved my head about on the pillow.

'Well, you know where to find me if you need me. My work number's in the book. Or you could always go over the road. Steven's mum, she'll be there. They're in the book, as well,' added Nan.

I clutched at the duvet, bunching it up to my chin. I knew she meant well, but why couldn't she just *go*?

'I'll be back for lunch. But if you get hungry, there's plenty of stuff in the fridge. Just help yourself to whatever you want.'

There was the sound of footsteps across the room, then a swish as the curtains were pulled back. Brutal beams of sunlight came flooding in. I curled myself into a protesting ball. Why is it they always have to be messing with the curtains? Mum's the same.

Duffy, it's time to get up! Tramp, creak, swish, *bang*.

'There!' I heard Nan's footsteps treading back again. 'That's better! Let some daylight in.'

I didn't want daylight. I just wanted to be left alone!

'I hope when I get back,' said Nan, 'I'll see you up and about . . . and don't go hunching over that machine! A lovely day like this, you ought to be out in the fresh air. I'll tell you what—'

Go. Go! *Go!*

'If you need something to do, that grass needs cutting. That would save me a job. Save my poor old legs. I just mention it,' said Nan. 'You don't have to if you don't want to. But it would be a nice gesture.'

I screwed my face up, against the pillow.

'Well, then. I'd best be off. I'll see you later. Take care!'

I heard her footsteps disappearing down the stairs and along the hall. I heard the front door open and close. Then the beep of the remote: car door clunking shut, car backing out of the drive. At last! She was gone! Now perhaps I could get back to sleep.

It was all I wanted to do: just *sleep*. I could sleep right the way through summer, if only they'd let me. Sleep until Mum came back with Charlotte, and the nightmare was over.

If ever it was.

Sometimes nightmares just go on and on. Even I couldn't sleep for ever.

I turned, and punched at the pillow. Sunlight streamed through the window, bright egg-yolk yellow.

Yeeurgh! I yanked the duvet back over my head but I could still feel it, boring into me. Why couldn't it be winter? Black clouds, grey skies, and the rain pelting down. Drumming on the roof, sloshing in the gutters. Drip-drip-dripping off the trees and the bushes. And I would hibernate in my nest and no one could get at me.

Under the duvet, I began to sweat. I stuck out a leg; and then the other. I desperately didn't want to get up. There was nothing to get up *for*. Unless Mum had replied to our e-mail? She might have done.

I bleared at the clock on the bedside table. Ten minutes to nine. That meant it was ... I worked backwards on my fingers. Ten to one, where Mum was. Middle of the night; she would be asleep. But it had been five o'clock in the afternoon when Nan and I had sent our e-mail. Ten in the morning for Mum. She would have been at the hospital with Charlotte; sometimes, I knew, she stayed there all night. Other times she drove back to Auntie Marje's. Sixty-three miles! I'd measured it on the map. But sixty-three miles isn't anything in America. If Mum had driven back, she would have picked up the e-mail and sent one in return. That would be worth getting up for.

Maybe. Maybe not. It would all depend what the news was.

Slowly, I crawled out of bed, pulled on jeans and a T-shirt and went through to the spare room, which is where Nan keeps the computer. *The machine*. It sits there, on a table, in solitary splendour. Just a vase of artificial flowers to keep it company.

'Makes it look a bit more human, somehow.' She slays me, Nan does! The things she says. She makes me laugh even when I'm not in a particularly laughing kind of mood. Which that summer I mostly wasn't.

My heart did a bit of a leap when I saw there was an e-mail, but then I saw that it was from Auntie Marje, not Mum.

Dear Duffy,

Got your message! Your mum is spending most of her time at the hospital just at the moment. Charlotte's having tests and she wants to be with her. But I spoke to her on the phone just a short while ago and she sounded cheerful and sends you and Nan all her love. She will e-mail SOON.

In the meanwhile, Charlotte sends hugs and kisses. Your mum says she is being a very brave girl and she was glad to hear that you are also bearing up. It was a great weight off her mind, knowing that she can rely on you.

I am going to visit with Charlotte tomorrow and will report. Lots of love to you and Nan,

XXX, Auntie Marje.

An e-mail from Auntie Marje was better than nothing, though it was Mum I really wanted to hear from. What I would have liked more than anything was to hear her voice. Well, it wasn't what I would have liked more than *anything*. What I would have liked more than anything was for life to go back to normal. But as it never could, I'd have settled for just the sound of her voice.

Now that I was at the computer I felt a strong temptation to stay and hunch, except that Nan had expressly told me not to. I mean, OK, she wasn't to know, but it would have made me feel guilty, being as this was her house and she was putting up with me for the whole of the summer. I have this great relationship with Nan, we get on really well, but she's never been the clingy sort. She's never slobbered over us. It's always been, you have your lives, I have mine. I reckoned it was pretty good of her to take me in. It didn't seem fair to go and hunch while her back was turned.

I switched the computer off and wandered downstairs in search of breakfast. I'm not one of those macho types who thinks it's girly to be domesticated. I can boil an egg! I can do them scrambled or in omelettes as well. But just right now I couldn't be bothered with food. I dumped three slices of bread in the toaster, downed a glass of milk, then took the toast out into the garden. Nan was right, the grass did need cutting. Maybe I'd shift myself and do it for her. As a surprise. 'Cos she wouldn't be expecting it, that was for sure. She'd expect me to still be slobbing in bed or sitting at the computer. At *the machine*.

I finished the toast and set off to fetch the mower from the garden shed. As I was trundling it out, I heard a voice call 'Hi!'. It was so unexpected it made me jump.

I spun round. A girl was sitting astride the wall at the end of the garden. She waved at me.

'Hi!'

'H-hi,' I said.

'Are you Duffy?'

'Yes,' I said. 'Who are y-y-y—'

'Me? I'm Alice!'

The dreaded Alice. Alice who had mad fits. Alice who threatened to strangle people. She didn't *look* very terrible. She looked kind of cute. Long blonde hair pulled back into a ponytail. Blue eyes, round face, dimples when she smiled. Of course, looks could be deceiving, I realized that. I mean, take me. I don't exactly come across as an alien; not at first glance. It's only when I open my mouth you discover that I'm from another planet.

'Alice Gregory. I live here.' She flapped a hand over her shoulder. 'My dad's a friend of your nan. They go to the same church. You're here for the whole of the holidays, right?'

I nodded.

'Where's your mum and dad?' said Alice.

I felt like saying, 'No business of yours.' Needless to say, I didn't. I'm always *thinking* these things; but I almost never give voice to them. I said, 'Th – th – th—' and my head went into overdrive. Sometimes I feel it might almost jerk itself right off.

'I'm only asking out of curiosity,' said Alice. 'They never tell me things! I only knew you were coming

16

because I heard Dad telling Mum. If I didn't keep my ears open, I'd never have a clue what was going on. They have these conversations, *pas devant les enfants*. Do yours ever say that?'

Bemused, I shook my head.

'It's French,' said Alice. Like I didn't know. *'Not in front of the children*. And, *little pitchers have big ears*. That's another one. As if we're about ten years old! It's because of my sister. Have you got a sister?'

I nodded; even more bemused. What was this? The third degree? I'd only just met this girl!

'Is she here with you?' said Alice.

I said, 'N-no. She's with my m-mum. In Am-m-merica.'

'Oh?' Alice cocked her head. Obviously waiting for more. But it wasn't anything to do with her!

'My sister's called Sarah,' she said. 'What's yours?'

'Ch-Charlotte.'

'Charlotte. That's pretty! I like that. How old is she?'

'She's th-three.'

'Mine's fourteen, but you'd never know it. She behaves more like ten. It's not her fault, she can't help it. But then they treat *me* like ten, and I hate it when they do that. I really hate it! I hate her, too.'

I guess I must have looked a bit taken aback. Alice gave this mad cackle and said, 'You should see your face!' She let her jaw hang slack. (I quickly checked my mouth was closed.) 'It's all right! She hates me, I hate her.' The way she said it, you'd have thought it was the most natural thing in the world. 'And anyway,' said Alice, 'she hated me first. She hated me the minute she set eyes on me.'

'W-what, when you were j-just b-babies?' I said.

'No! When they adopted me. She was adopted first, so she got all resentful. She told me, when I came, that she hated me. I don't care!' Alice tossed her head. I watched in fascination as her ponytail swished to and fro. 'Doesn't bother *me*. I can look after myself!'

I swallowed. I was reluctantly beginning to wonder if Steven's mum might not have been right about Alice, after all. She might have a face like a flower, but she seemed to harbour some very violent emotions.

'So what is your mum doing in America?' she said. 'I hope you don't think I'm being nosy.' She smiled her dimpled smile. These two little pits appeared in her cheeks. 'I'm just interested! Why she's over there and you're here. And where's your dad? Is he with them, or is he somewhere else? You don't have to tell me,' she said, 'if you don't want. Not if you think I'm being nosy.'

I did, as a matter of fact, but I found myself telling her anyway. Goodness knows why; it's not something I would normally talk about. But I munched and I chewed, and my right arm shot out and punched the air, then went into a spasm and wouldn't come out of it, and Alice sat on the wall and listened, with her blue eyes wide.

I gave her the whole bit, all about Mum and Dad splitting up, about Charlotte being sick and local people raising money so that Mum could take her to America for an operation. I'd never actually told anyone else. At school I didn't have to, because most everyone knew.

18

They ran the story in the local paper, so it was common knowledge round our way. Steven hadn't asked and I wouldn't have told him if he had. I still didn't know why I'd told Alice, only that she seemed to expect me to

'When do you think she'll have it?' she said. 'The operation?'

I said, 'S-soon. If they d-decide they c-can do it.'

'When do you think they'll know?'

I shrugged, and shook my head.

'Scary,' said Alice.

So scary that I mostly tried not to think about it. When I did think about it—

My right arm suddenly shot out again and punched the air. It's quite embarrassing when this happens, though I would say more for other people than for me. I guess by now I've got used to it. But with other people, they look away really fast. Either that, or if they're just dumb kids they snigger or take the piss.

Alice didn't do any of those things. She just sat there, solemnly gazing at me out of these very clear blue eyes.

'Why do you keep doing this?' she said, shooting out an arm. 'And this—' She twitched. 'Is it muscle spasms?'

'No,' I said, 'it's a t-touch of the T-Tourette's.'

Most people haven't even heard of Tourette's. My nan hadn't, for a start. Not until they discovered I had it, that is. When Mum first told her, Nan said, '*Cigarette* syndrome? What's that when it's at home?' Mum and me used to make jokes about it . . . Duffy's cigarette

19

syndrome. Dad never did. Dad was always too ashamed of me.

'I'm a bit of a n-n-n-*odd*ball,' I said.

'So'm I,' said Alice. 'I bet you're not as odd as me. Everyone'll tell you, I'm barking mad . . . woof, woof!' She sounded almost as if she were proud of it.

I said, 'I don't exp-pect you know what T-Tourette's is.'

'I do, too!' said Alice. 'I once saw this film about someone who was pretending to have it. They kept shouting out rude words all the time. Do you shout out rude words?'

I said no, I mostly just munched and twitched.

'That's a pity,' she said. 'Rude words would be more fun. Bottoms! Boobs! Bum!'

'Arse'ole,' I said, not to be outdone.

'Balls! Bollocks!'

'Pantyhose!'

'*Pantyhose?*' She giggled. 'That's not rude!'

I said, 'I know. I c-couldn't think of anything else on the sp-pur of the moment.'

'I can think of loads,' said Alice.

I believed her. I just bet she could!

She shuffled along the wall. 'D'you want to come and sit up here?'

I wouldn't have minded. This was the first time in my entire life I'd ever come across anyone who knew about Tourette's! Who wasn't fazed by it. Just took it for granted. But then I thought of Nan's grass, waiting to be cut.

'B-best not,' I said. 'I've got to c-c-c—' I stopped. *'Mow the lawn!* For my nan.'

'I'll help!'

She slithered down off the wall. Other people might have waited to be asked before slithering into someone else's garden, but Alice didn't seem to be like other people. Any more than I was. We were both of us oddballs! I found the thought strangely comforting.

I yanked the lawn mower into position. It's one of those old-fashioned jobs, without a motor.

'We can push it together,' said Alice.

It was pretty hard work, with both of us pushing. It would actually have been far easier to do it on my own, but I didn't like to say so in case she took offence and went away. All the time we're mowing she's talking nineteen to the dozen. She talks nonstop.

'Your nan works in the Fashion Box, doesn't she? I've seen her in there. She always looks dead smart! Not like my nan. Do you want to take a look at my nan?'

I couldn't honestly have said that I did, but she seemed to want me to. She crept up to the wall and peered over.

'There!' She put her finger to her lips and beckoned at me. 'That's my nan over there, see?'

I took a look, just to please her. All I saw was this old woman in a baggy dress, hanging out some washing. She looked just like any other old woman, as far as I could see. I mean, she was obviously a lot older than my nan, and a bit grouchy-looking, in fact quite disagreeable, really; but nothing out of the ordinary.

'That's Granny Gregory,' said Alice. 'Our dad's mum. She lives with us. She's grungy! She's really mean to my mum. It's 'cos of our dad being her only child. She didn't have him until she was forty. That's late to have a baby, that is,' said Alice. 'I bet your nan isn't anywhere near as old!'

'She is quite old,' I said. 'She's going to retire soon. She's nearly sixty.'

'That's nothing,' said Alice. 'Granny Gregory's over eighty. Look, there's my sister Sarah. Do you think she's pretty?'

'Um – well.' What did she want me to say? A girl had come out of the house and was helping the old woman hang clothes. She was tall and thin and a bit stooped, with lank dark hair that fell over her eyes. And no, I didn't think she was pretty.

'She doesn't look like you,' was all I said.

'Well, she wouldn't, would she?' said Alice. 'I told you . . . we're adopted. That's why she's pretty and I'm not.'

I didn't say anything. To be honest, I thought she was just fishing for compliments.

'Don't you think she's pretty?' Alice turned to look at me. 'Dad does. He says that I'm plain and Sarah's beautiful.'

I frowned. That was nonsense! No one could be prettier than Alice, with her bluebell eyes and little round face.

'Our dad says that beauty comes from within. He says

if you have beautiful thoughts you'll be beautiful to look at. But if you have *bad* thoughts—' She stopped.

I said, 'What s-sort of b-bad thoughts?'

'Just bad,' muttered Alice. The expression on her face made me feel uncomfortable. Did she mean bad like . . . throttling people? '*Bad*,' she said. '*Ugly*.'

'We all have b-bad th-thoughts at t-times,' I said.

'Yeah?' She studied me a moment, like she was debating the truth of this remark.

'Anyway. What does your d-dad do?' I said. I reckoned if she could ask questions, so could I.

'My dad? He runs a care home,' said Alice. 'Christian care home. Are you a Christian?'

I hesitated.

'It's all right if you're not.'

'I th-think I am,' I said. It's something I'm never quite sure of.

'I'm not,' said Alice. 'I'm not anything. I'm a heathen. I still have to go to church, but I don't pray. When everyone else is praying, I think up poems in my head. And when they're singing hymns, I just mouth the words. Or sometimes I sing different ones. Ones I've made up. Like—'

She suddenly broke into unmelodious song. She couldn't sing in tune, that was for sure!

'*The church's one foundation*
Is Playtex Wonderbra.
It lifteth and supporteth,
From near and from afar!

23

'— I think it would be hypocritical to sing words if you don't believe in them, don't you?'

'Y-yeah,' I said. 'I s'pose it would.'

'Anyway,' said Alice, 'that's what I think. It's quite difficult, not being a Christian when you live with them all around you. My mum's one, too. That's how they met, being Christians. Now they work together in the care home. They go to your nan's church; did you know that? That's why I asked if you were a Christian. I like to know where I stand.' She paused. 'My dad's in the choir, he's quite important. He could have been a priest if he'd wanted to. When he was younger. But they don't have priests now; not in his church. It's *evangelical*.'

I racked my brains for something to say. Nothing came. Absolutely nothing! I wasn't used to having long conversations with people.

This particular conversation seemed to have ground to a halt. It was Alice who got it going again.

'Do you like kittens?' she said. 'We've got some indoors. Four of them! They're really cute. You could come and see them, if you want. Would you like to? We'll just get the grass cut first, before your nan comes back. Then you can come round.'

There is a lot of grass in Nan's garden. In fact, it would be true to say that it's almost all grass. We were just doing the last strip when Nan came through the back door.

'Oh. Alice!' she said. 'So you've met.'

I explained that Alice was helping me with the grass.

24

'Well, that's very kind of her,' said Nan. She said it sort of . . . guardedly. Not as if she really thought it was kind at all.

'I'd better be getting back for lunch,' said Alice.

'Yes, you had,' said Nan. 'It's nearly half-past one.'

'See you, Oddball!' Alice flapped a hand and swung herself back over the wall. Her head came bobbing up from the other side. 'Knickers, bottom, boobs!'

'B-bumhole!' I shouted.

'Pigswill! Don't forget the kittens. Come for tea!'

Alice disappeared.

'What was that all about?' said Nan. 'All the knickers and the bums?'

'It was just a j-joke,' I said.

'Why did she call you Oddball?'

'That was a j-joke, too.'

Nan said, 'Hm!' and shook her head. 'I wish she wouldn't climb over the wall like that. She'll bring the whole thing down, if she's not careful. What did she mean about the kittens?'

'She's got some,' I said. 'She said I could go and see them, if I wanted. Is that OK?'

'I suppose so,' said Nan. She wasn't as enthusiastic as I'd thought she'd be. Considering she was the one who'd wanted me to find a friend. 'What about Steven?' she said.

What about him? 'I'd rather see the kittens,' I said.

'You can see the kittens. I've no objection to that,' said Nan. 'But Alice is a very strange child. You don't want to go getting too close. And, Duffy! Please don't climb over the wall. Go to the front door. All right? I know it means walking round the block but I don't think Alice's father would be very pleased to have strange boys suddenly appearing in his garden. He's a lovely man,' she said, 'Alice's father. How he copes with that girl I do not know.'

'He's a Christian,' I said.

Nan sniffed. 'So am I, but I couldn't cope with her! The man's a saint, if you ask me. I've known him for years, long before he adopted the girls. They just moved house, a few months ago. I was so thrilled! Having him just a stone's throw away. But that Alice,' she said. 'She's a handful!'

3

'I'm going to go and see the kittens, then,' I said to Nan.

'*Round the front*,' said Nan.

Dutifully, I went round the front. Up the road, make a left; tramp tramp, make a left; tramp tramp until I came to Alice's house. Climbing the wall would have been a whole lot easier.

'Hi, Oddball!' Alice stood at the door, grinning. 'Why d'you come round this way?'

I told her that Nan had said I'd got to. 'She said your d-dad wouldn't like me climbing over the w-w-w—'

'Wall,' said Alice. 'Why not?'

'She said it might f-fall down.'

'Course it wouldn't!' said Alice. 'I climb over all the time.'

I wondered why she would do that. Why would she climb into Nan's garden *all the time*?

'Like if I kick a ball, or something? Take too long to keep going round the front. And anyway, your nan mightn't be there. Don't want to have to wait all day, do I?'

'I guess not.' It occurred to me that Alice was what Nan would call 'a law unto herself'.

'Well, come on!' She gave me a tug. I stepped through, obediently, into the hall. Something else that occurred to me: she was quite a bossy piece. Not that I minded. I don't like being pushed around, but Alice could get away with a bit of bossing. Something to do with blue eyes and dimples, maybe.

The hall that she was tugging me along was like a cavern, vast and dark. The house was far larger than Nan's; much older, too. Nan's is just a little box, very square and neat.

'Down here,' said Alice. She led the way along the cavern towards a door at the end. 'This –' She threw open the door and stood back, with a flourish. Inviting me to marvel. 'This is our kitchen!'

I knew that something was expected of me, but all I could think to say, in feeble tones, was, 'Ah'.

I was a bit gobsmacked, to tell the truth. I'd never seen anything like it! It was like something out of Victorian England. Like old brown photographs of stone sinks and skivvies. The sink wasn't *actually* stone, but it was pretty ancient. The cupboards were all rickety; not fitted, like Nan's. There was a long wooden table down the centre, and a creaking fan high up on one wall. The floor was just, like, bare slabs, with a few old rugs scattered over it. Way out!

In one corner of this room that time forgot stood Granny Gregory, all wrapped in black like an old witch. She was stirring something on the stove. Something in a big pot. Wing of bat and tongue of newt. I thought that if I looked it would be all green and bubbling.

Sarah was also there, sitting at the table, stolidly peeling cloves of garlic. She and Granny Gregory both turned as I came in. They studied me, Sarah, like I was some kind of no-neck monster from outer space; Granny Gregory like she was wondering if I might make a useful addition to her witch's brew. Neither of them said a word.

It was a bit disconcerting. I mean, I'm used to people thinking I'm odd when I twitch or jerk, but not when I'm just standing there.

Alice waved a hand.

'This is my nan,' she said. 'This is my sister. And these—' she squatted down, by the side of the table '— are my kittens.'

Sarah came suddenly to life.

'*My* kittens!'

She pushed back her chair and rushed round to Alice. 'Minnie is *my* cat!'

'Our cat,' said Alice.

'My cat! She's my cat!'

'*Our* cat!'

'My cat!'

The two of them sat back on their heels, glowering. For just a moment, I thought they were going to start in on each other. I thought Alice might be about to go into her strangling mode. And then the cat, under the table, made a chirruping sound, and both girls sprang into action.

'Minn*ee*!'

'Min!'

They dived on her. Sarah got there first and snatched her up.

'She's mine!'

'Ours!'

'M—'

'*Stop that!*' The old witch at the stove suddenly came to life. She hammered on the wall with her ladle. 'Stop it, the pair of you! I knew it was a mistake, bringing an animal into the house. I said so right from the beginning. I knew it would cause problems. Alice, leave your sister alone!'

Alice said, 'I'm not touching her!'

'Well, don't.'

'I'm not!'

'There'll be trouble,' said Granny Gregory.

'See?' Sarah pulled a face. I wouldn't have been surprised if she'd added, 'Sah, sah, sah!'

'Well, anyway—' Alice said it sullenly. I couldn't altogether blame her '— those are the kittens. *Our* kittens. It's all right, you can touch them,' she said. 'She won't scratch. Minnie, I mean.' She looked hard at Sarah as she said it.

'B-best not d-disturb them,' I said.

'They're mine,' muttered Sarah.

'You say that about everything!' yelled Alice. She grabbed hold of me. 'Come upstairs and I'll show you my room. *My* room!' She glared at Sarah. 'Come and see some of *my things*. Without *her* around.'

She tugged me back out into the passage. Sarah called after us, from the kitchen doorway.

'They're mine, they're mine! Bluuuurgh!' She stuck out her tongue. Alice shouted, 'Knickerspantsbumhole!' and made a rude gesture with a finger.

'Just because she was here first,' she grumbled. 'Minnie isn't her cat, and the kittens aren't hers, either! But they always take her side.'

'Who? Your m-mum and dad?' I said.

'Everyone! *Pooooor* Sarah,' crooned Alice. 'Nasty, hateful, horrible Alice!' She slapped at herself. Quite hard. Hard enough to make me wince. And to leave a red weal on her face. 'You stop that! Don't you hit your sister! *Poooor* little Sarah . . . everyone's got to be nice to Sarah!'

She hurtled up the stairs, three at a time. I hurtled after her.

'This is it. This is my room.' She flung open a door. A big notice was stuck on it: PRIVATE SPACE. TRESPASSERS WILL BE PROSECUTED. '*My* room. Where *she's* not allowed. It's smaller than hers 'cos she had to have first choice. But I don't care! This one's mine and she can't come in it. Look! Do you like my picture?'

She pointed, proudly, at a picture on the wall.

'Um . . .' I stared at it, wondering what to say. It looked like a page torn out of a kids' book. It was a picture of an old-fashioned girl, with long fair hair and a blue dress, peering down a rabbit hole. Pretty yucky, to be honest.

'Um . . . y-yeah. It's n-nice,' I said. 'What is it?'

'Alice going down the rabbit hole. Alice in *Wonderland*,' said Alice.

'Oh. Yeah!' I nodded, trying to appear knowledgeable and obviously not succeeding. Alice looked at me, sternly.

'Don't tell me you haven't *read* it?' she said.

'W-well . . . n-no. N-not exactly,' I said. 'I mean, I know what it's about, of course.'

'So I should hope,' said Alice. 'It's a *classic*. I've read it ten times. At least! *Alice in Wonderland* and *Through the Looking Glass*. They're my favourite books. I can't *believe* you haven't read them!'

I'd definitely gone down a notch or two in her estimation. It bothered me. I don't know why. Trying to regain a bit of lost ground I said, 'My favourite's *The L-Lord of the R-Rings*.'

Oh, really? Big deal!

'Haven't read it,' said Alice.

Earnestly, I told her that she didn't know what she was missing.

'Why?' said Alice. 'Is it good?'

'B-brilliant,' I said.

'Oh! Well.'

There was a pause; then she went back to the picture.

'My mum gave me that picture,' she said. 'My *real* mum. 'Cos of my name being Alice. It's all I've got to remember her by. See, she and my dad weren't married, so she had to give me up. She didn't want to, but her family made her. 'Cos they were very posh, and my dad, he was an artist and they looked down on him. They thought he was beneath them. So my mum wasn't allowed to keep me. And now all I've got is my picture. Which is why,' said Alice, 'it means so much to me.'

Phew! What a relief! That I hadn't said anything bad about it. Naturally if her mum had given it to her it would make it precious no matter how tacky it was.

'I'm really surprised you haven't read the books,' said Alice. 'I would have thought everyone would have read them.'

I would have thought everyone would have read *The Lord of the Rings*, if it came to that.

'I could lend them to you,' she said, 'if you like.'

I made a mumbling sound. I don't mean to be sexist, but I don't usually read books about girls. I find them a bit – well. Tame. To tell the truth. A bit soppy. All about love. Or about girls doing girly things. Making friends and falling out and making up again. On the other hand, I'd got to admit, Alice herself wasn't soppy. She wasn't tame, either. She was quite fierce. Far fiercer than I am!

'Would you like me to?' she said.

I said, 'Yeah, why not?'

'I'll lend you mine, then you can lend me yours. That'd be fair, wouldn't it?'

I agreed that it would, while secretly hoping she'd forget. I'm not the world's greatest reader, to tell the honest truth. I'm more of a computer person.

Alice was looking again at her picture. 'She's going

down the rabbit hole, see? I go down the rabbit hole, sometimes.'

'You go d-down the r-r-*rabbit* hole?' I said.

'Y-y-yes!' said Alice. She giggled. 'Knickers!'

'P-*pants*!'

'Bumhole!'

'How do you g-get d-down there?' I said.

'I make myself *small*, like she did.' Alice threw herself on to the bed and curled into a ball. 'Then I go into the hole, and I'm not here any more. I disappear! It's like in *Star Trek* . . . I go into a time warp. Different plane of existence. Know what I mean?'

I said, 'Mmm . . . I s'ppose.' I was still puzzling over what she'd said. How could she possibly make herself small enough to go down a rabbit hole? She couldn't! It didn't make any sense.

'You don't believe me, do you?' She sprang up from the bed. 'Come on, and I'll show you!'

She yanked me out of the bedroom and back down the stairs. Bang, wallop, two at a time. She never seemed to go anywhere at a walk. It was always a frantic rush.

We raced back along the cavernous hall and into the kitchen. Granny Gregory was still there, still stirring her pot at the stove, but Sarah had disappeared. Watching television in the back room from the sound of things.

'Let's take the kittens with us!' cried Alice. 'Give them a bit of fresh air. Here!' She picked up the basket and thrust it at me. 'You carry them!'

What could I do? I stumbled out into the garden with

the cat basket. I could feel these malevolent eyes watching me from the stove.

'Put it here,' said Alice.

I set the basket on the lawn and all the kittens sat up and yawned. There were four of them: two black and white, one ginger, one striped.

'Won't they g-get lost?' I said.

'No! Minnie'll watch over them. She won't let them go anywhere. If they wander off, she'll just pick them up in her mouth and bring them back again. She's a *very good* mother,' said Alice. 'Now come and see my rabbit hole!'

She went zooming off down the garden. I followed, watching over my shoulder as the kittens, one by one, came wriggling out of their basket. I supposed they'd be all right. I supposed Alice knew what she was talking about. I've never had any pets. Dad wasn't into animals, and now we're in a flat there isn't enough room. I have thought of asking Mum if we could have an aquarium. Tropical fish! I'd like that.

'Here!' Alice was waving at me, impatiently. 'This is where I go, see?'

She dived beneath a tangle of undergrowth and disappeared from view. I pushed after her, through a kind of prickly tunnel hollowed out among the brambles. I found her crouched at the entrance to a hole which some animal had dug in the sandy pit between some old tree roots, hard up against the wall. Whatever sort of animal it was, it certainly wasn't a rabbit.

'That's a fox earth!' I said.

'It's a rabbit hole,' said Alice.

It wasn't a rabbit hole; it was a fox earth. I bit my lip, however, and didn't say anything. I had the feeling it might not be wise to argue with her.

Alice sighed. 'I *pretend* that it's a rabbit hole. OK? And when I'm sitting here, like this—' she made herself small, tucking her knees up to her chin '— that's when I can't be got at. If ever you see me like this, it means I'm down the hole. Got it?'

I swallowed. 'Y-yeah.'

'That's all right, then.' Alice scrambled back out. 'I just wanted you to know. In case you come looking for me ever, and that's where I am.'

'Right.' I nodded. 'R-right!'

'Even *she* knows not to get at me when I'm down the rabbit hole.'

Alice hoisted herself up on to the wall. I was about to swing up beside her when I remembered Nan and her feelings about people climbing on walls. So I waved a hand at the fox earth and said, 'We've got a f-f-f—'

'Fox,' said Alice. 'I know. I've seen it. I think it used to live here, and now it's made another home for itself. I th—' She broke off as a loud wail came from the other end of the garden.

'Who's let my kittens out?'

'I have!' Alice leapt off the wall and went roaring back, through the brambles and across the grass. 'It's a lovely day and they need some fresh air. And they are *not* your kittens!'

The kittens were in little heaps on the lawn. They seemed quite happy. So did Minnie, who was sitting in her basket, washing herself. But Sarah, in a frenzy, had begun plucking them up.

'They're my kittens and they're not old enough! They'll get *lost*. Leave them alone! Just leave them alone! I hate you! I hate you! I hate you!'

Her voice rose in an anguished crescendo.

'Hate you, too!' screamed Alice.

'Alice!' A woman had suddenly appeared from out of the kitchen door. 'What's going on?'

'It's her!' sobbed Sarah. 'She's taken my kittens!'

'I didn't *take* them.' Alice said it scornfully. 'I put them in the garden to get some fresh air.'

'Well, I'm taking them back in again!'

Sarah scooped up the last of the kittens and plonked it in the basket. The woman said, 'Alice, I wish you wouldn't keep upsetting Sarah. You know your father doesn't like it when she cries.'

Alice tossed her head. Her ponytail swished, angrily. She marched back indoors, leaving me on my own, feeling foolish.

'I'm sorry.' The woman looked at me, in a helpless sort of way. She was all woolly and fluffy, with fuzzy grey hair and a pair of granny glasses that kept slipping down her nose. She put me in mind, for some reason, of a sheep. 'I'm Alice's mum,' she said. 'You must be—'

'D-d-d—'

'Oddball!' Alice's voice came screeching out. 'I've

invited him to tea!' Her head bobbed round the door. 'Are you coming, or what?'

I hesitated.

'No, please!' Alice's mum, the sheep lady, ushered me ahead of her. 'Don't mind the girls, they're always at loggerheads.'

I thought, *loggerheads*. Knickers, pantyhose, *loggerheads*. I stored it up for future use. I may not be the world's most avid reader, but I do like new words. I like to toss them into a conversation, just casually.

We went through to the kitchen. Sarah was under the table, making little sniffly sounds over the kittens.

'Sarah, darling, please don't cry,' begged the sheep lady. 'Your dad will be in any minute.'

Alice banged herself down, scowling, on to a chair.

'Alice! *Manners*,' said the sheep lady. 'Duffy, take a seat.'

Somewhat nervously, I sat down next to Alice. Sarah, still sniffling, slid sideways on to a chair opposite.

'Dry your eyes,' pleaded the sheep lady. 'There's a good girl! You don't want your dad to see you like that, do you?'

'Yes, she does!' yelled Alice. 'She wants to get me into trouble!'

'You're a fine one to talk about trouble,' said the old witch in the corner. Witch woman and sheep lady. I forced myself to stop thinking of them like that. They were Alice's gran and Alice's mum.

Alice's gran leaned across the table. She put her face right up close to Alice and hissed, 'You're the one that's trouble, my girl!'

I thought that was a bit unfair, though I accepted it might have been wrong of her to take the kittens into the garden. Not that they had come to any harm, but I had this feeling she had only done it to annoy Sarah. In the meanwhile, it didn't look like being much of a fun meal, what with Alice scowling and Sarah snivelling and their mum all fretting and anxious. Not to mention Granny Gregory, hunched up like an old bat. I began to wish I hadn't come. I don't usually get myself into these sort of social situations; I'm far better with the computer.

'Here's your dad, now,' said Alice's mum. She sent a warning glance at Alice. 'Just remember, he's had a hard day. I don't want you upsetting him!'

The kitchen door crashed open and a whirlwind blew in. Ginger-haired and bearded, and about seven foot tall.

'Dad!' Sarah flew at him. She fastened her arms round his waist and pressed her head into his midriff. Alice instantly followed suit.

'Dad, Dad!' And then *she* fastened her arms round him – as best she could, with Sarah having got in first – and started on the head pressing bit.

I don't know why, but it made me uncomfortable, seeing Alice behave like Sarah. It seemed . . . wrong, somehow. Out of character. But I couldn't have said why. I mean, what did I know? Maybe this was the way that normal people behaved with their dads.

'Well, well, well! And who have we here?'

A great jovial voice boomed round the kitchen. Alice giggled. Sarah said, '*She* brought him.'

Alice's mum said, 'Sarah! Duffy is our guest ... Norman, this is Mrs Chambers' boy. Alice invited him to tea.'

'Did she so? Quite right, too! Pleased to make your acquaintance, young man!'

I found my hand being pumped up and down in this big bear-like grip. I began to relax a bit. Up until now, I'd been feeling distinctly that I was surplus to requirements. So to speak. Sarah obviously resented me, I'd sent the sheep lady into a nervous fluster, and the witch woman, I got the feeling, would automatically distrust anyone that Alice brought home. Her dad was the only one who made me feel welcome.

Alice's dad was great. All through tea he kept up this stream of really corny jokes, which meant I didn't have to do any talking; just laugh. Laughing is easy! Even I can manage that. Alice laughed, too; loudly and uproariously. Sarah sat next to her dad, snuggled against him in a way that struck me as being somewhat childish, but maybe Sarah was rather childish. It was hard to believe she was fourteen.

At the end of the meal Alice's dad said, 'How would you like to join us on a family outing, young master Duffy? On Saturday. Magical Mystery Tour.'

Alice shrieked and clapped her hands. 'Magical Mystery!'

I looked at her, oddly. The way Alice behaved in the presence of her dad was quite different from the way she behaved when she was on her own with me. I guessed he must be a pretty big influence in her life. I guessed he would be a pretty big influence in anyone's life. He was like . . . kingsize. A great splurge of a man. I had to stop myself comparing him all the time with my dad.

Alice's mum gave a little flutey laugh and said, 'Norman and his magical mysteries! He's famous for them, Duffy.'

'So how about it?' the big voice bellowed out. 'Think your gran would entrust you to us?'

I grinned. 'I r-reckon!'

'Then it's a date,' said Alice's dad.

4

As soon as I got back to Nan's I rushed upstairs to check the e-mails. To see if there was one from Mum. There wasn't.

'Too early,' said Nan. 'She'll be at the hospital. She'll most likely stay over for the next few days.'

'Yeah.' I tried not to sound too dejected; I knew that Nan was probably right.

'Don't worry! Your Auntie Marje will let us know if there's any news. Now, don't you go hunching over that machine,' said Nan. 'You come downstairs with me. We'll have a cup of tea.'

Nan's always having cups of tea. She is addicted to tannic acid! I bet if you could see inside her lungs they'd be coated with the stuff.

I tore myself away from the computer and trailed back downstairs after her. We sat at the kitchen table, Nan with her tea (dark brown and bitter), me with an orange juice. I don't go much for tea, and Mum doesn't like me to drink Coke, or anything fizzy and sweet. She has this theory it's bad for my Tourette's. She claims the few times she's let me have Coke I've hardly been able to speak for twitching.

42

'We mustn't brood,' said Nan. 'Your mum's relying on us.'

'But we c-can't d-*do* anything,' I said.

'We can try and keep cheerful, that's one thing we can do. Your mum's got enough on her plate.'

I didn't quite see how us keeping cheerful was going to help Mum, all those thousands of miles away. But I dunno! There may be something in the power of thought.

'Tell you what,' said Nan. 'Steven's mum came into the shop this morning. She suggested you might like to go out with them this Saturday. They're going up to town. That would be fun, wouldn't it?'

I said, 'I can't, on Saturday.'

'Why not? What else are you doing?'

I explained how Alice's dad had invited me on a magical mystery tour. Nan said, 'Oh! Well. If it was Alice's dad.'

'It was,' I said.

'That's all right. I wouldn't want you getting too close to Alice. Not if I'm to be honest. But if it was her dad . . .' Nan cradled her tea cup in her hands. Her expression had gone all soppy. All soft focus. 'He's a lovely man, Alice's dad! Big Norm.' She gave this little laugh. Almost girlish. 'That's what we call him, in the church. Big Norm! If he was the one who asked you, then you go! But just watch out for that Alice. She's a right little so-and-so! If she was mine she'd feel the back of my hand, I can tell you.'

I looked at Nan, reprovingly. 'You're not allowed to hit children, these days.'

'No,' said Nan, 'more's the pity! A good clip round the ear is what that girl needs. She's got this temper on her, she gets in one of her tantrums she's like a wild thing. She's had her hands round Sarah's throat more than once. There's no controlling her.'

I frowned. I had this feeling that Alice was my friend; I shouldn't be listening while Nan talked about her like that. It was . . . disloyal.

'Oh, I know what you're thinking!' said Nan. 'Poor little Alice, looks like a little angel. Butter wouldn't melt in her mouth . . . You wait till you've seen her in one of her paddies! She and Sarah don't get along too well, but that's no excuse for flying out at her.'

'Why has everyone got it in for Alice and not for Sarah?' I said.

'Because Sarah's just the way she is and she can't help it,' said Nan. 'Alice should have a bit more control. And I haven't *got it in for her*. I just feel sorry for poor Norman. Everything thrown back in his face. All I'm saying . . .' said Nan, 'don't get too close. That's all. Now where are you off to? You're not going to go and hunch over that machine, are you?'

'Nan! I haven't been anywhere near it all day.'

'Oh! I suppose you're getting withdrawal symptoms? Why can't you just stay down here with me? Watch a bit of telly, for a change.'

I guessed she wanted me to keep her company. But I

didn't feel like watching television, and I didn't feel like more talking. Specially not if she was going to keep on about Alice.

'If you don't want to watch the telly, you could always sit and read a book,' said Nan.

I said, 'What b-book?'

'Any book! Are you telling me you haven't got a book? You ought to be ashamed of yourself! That's what these *computers* do.' She curled her lip. 'They frazzle your brain.'

I said, 'My b-brain's not frazzled.' A bit of it might be; the bit I use for speaking. And the bit that makes me twitch. But not the thinking part! And it's not because of the computer, anyway. It's to do with my genes.

'I suppose you haven't got *Alice in W-Wonderland*?' I said.

She hadn't, of course; Nan only reads big fat books with shiny covers.

'You could always join the library,' she called, as I went back upstairs. 'They'd have it in the library!'

' 'S all right,' I said. 'I can g-get it from Alice.'

Next morning, there was an e-mail. I picked it up after Nan had left for work. It was from Auntie Marje again, but she said that Mum had dictated it over the phone.

Duffy darling,
This is Mum! I'm staying with Charlotte in the hospital. I'll be here for the next few days.
   This morning we had the best news ever. They are going

45

ahead with the operation! They're planning to do it on Tuesday. It will be a while before we know whether it's been successful, but the doctors say there is a good chance. So isn't that great? I wanted you and Nan to know immediately!

No time for more right now, but lots of love and kisses from Mum and Charlotte.

I immediately rang Nan at work, to give her the news.

'It is g-good,' I said, 'isn't it? It-s g-good they're going ahead?'

'It's excellent!' said Nan. 'It means we've cleared the first hurdle.'

The second hurdle would be the operation itself; that would be the really big one. But I'd worry about that later. One thing at a time.

I poured myself a glass of milk and went out into the garden. Alice was there, sitting on the wall, swinging her legs in the sunshine.

'Hi, Oddball!'

I waved at her. 'Hi!'

'Bottom!'

'Bumhole!'

'Knickers!'

'L-loggerheads!'

'*Loggerheads?*' She giggled. 'Where'd you get that from?'

'Out the d-d-dictionary,' I said. 'It's all right for tomorrow, by the way. I can come on the m-mystery tour!'

'Oh. Good,' said Alice; but she didn't sound terribly

46

pleased. It crossed my mind that maybe she didn't really want me tagging along.

'I won't c-come if you'd r-rather I didn't.'

'You'll have to,' said Alice. 'He's invited you.'

'Yeah,' I said, 'but if you d-don't want me—'

'It's what *he* wants,' said Alice. 'Doesn't make any difference to me.'

'Well. OK. If you s-say so.' I swung myself up on the wall beside her. 'Where d'you r-reckon we'll go?'

'Dunno.' She shrugged. 'Wherever he decides. Where'd you used to go with your dad?'

I thought back, trying to remember. I hadn't been anywhere with Dad, very much. Dad was always too ashamed of me.

'P-places,' I said. And then, without quite meaning to, I burst out, 'Got an e-mail from my m-mum this morning. They're going to do the oper-r-r—'

'The operation?' said Alice. 'When?'

'T-Tuesday.'

'Oh, boy!' She looked at me, wide-eyed. 'Is it a mega one? Like you read about? One of those ones that goes on for hours?'

I kicked out. I really didn't want to talk about the operation. I wished I'd never brought it up in the first place.

'F-f-football!' I said.

'*Football?*' said Alice.

'I once went to a m-m-m—'

'Match.'

'With my d-d-dad.'

She didn't ask what going to a football match had to do with Charlotte's operation. For someone who was so up front, she could be quite sensitive when she wanted.

'I've got a football,' she said. 'Feel like a game?'

I nodded, gratefully. I didn't care what people said about Alice; I felt comfortable with her. There aren't many people I feel comfortable with. Mum; Nan; Charlotte. And now Alice. That's about all.

'C'mon, then!' She sprang down, on her side of the wall. 'They're all out. Mum and Dad are at work, and *she's* gone shopping with my gran ... S-s-s-*Sarah*!' She twitched. 'S-squitters and s-s-sick!'

'Earwax and pimples!'

'And great green grollies!' shouted Alice. 'On *toast*!'

Next day was Saturday. The day of the mystery tour. Nan doesn't work on Saturdays, so she walked round with me at ten o'clock. Personally, I think she just wanted the chance to see Big Norm. She was really gone on him! If she'd been a bit younger I'd almost have said she had a crush. But you don't get crushes, at Nan's age.

'When shall I expect you back?' she said.

'Now, now!' Alice's dad wagged a finger. 'That would be giving the game away! Who knows where we might end up? John o' Groats? Land's End?'

Nan gave a little trill of laughter. 'Sorry, I'm sure!'

Alice's mum said, 'Oh, Norman, of course we won't be going that far! No later than six, Mrs Chambers.'

Behind her back, Alice's dad pulled a face. Alice and Sarah both giggled. Just for a moment, I felt a bit sorry for Alice's mum. I know what it's like to have people pulling faces behind your back. It's something that happens to me all the time. They think you can't see them, but you can. On the other hand, I couldn't help feeling it was pretty dumb of her to have taken the suggestion seriously. I mean . . . John o' Groats or Land's End!

'One time,' said Sarah, 'we drove *all day*. Didn't we, Mum? We drove *all day long*.' She turned to Nan. 'We didn't get back until *midnight*.'

'Gone midnight,' said Alice.

'Mum was worried,' said Sarah. 'She thought Dad was overdoing it.'

'Yes, because he wouldn't let her drive,' said Alice. 'He never does. He—'

'*Alice! Sarah!*' Their dad had wrenched open the car door. 'That's enough! Both of you! Just get in and be quiet!' He grabbed Alice by the arm. Sarah didn't need any grabbing. She scuttled after Alice, fast as maybe. Their dad slammed the door behind them. There was a moment's uneasy silence.

'Well, I'll . . . love you and leave you, then,' said Nan. 'Have a good trip!'

Nan went off and I climbed into the back of the car with Alice and Sarah. Alice's mum was sitting in the front passenger seat. As we got in she turned round and said, 'You two girls! Have you both been to the loo?'

There was this pause. I didn't know which way to look. (To spare Alice's blushes, I mean.) I just couldn't believe her mum would say such a thing! Maybe if they'd been on their own; but in front of me. It was very belittling.

'Have you been?' she said.

'Been,' said Sarah.

'Don't need to,' said Alice.

'Are you sure? You know what happened last time!'

Alice scowled. 'Last time I *forgot*. This time I don't need to.'

'Well, all right. If you say so.' Her mum clunked her seat belt. 'But don't you start whining! If you've made a mistake, you'll just have to hold yourself.'

Alice had turned bright scarlet. I felt for her! I'd have been well embarrassed if my mum had talked to me like that in front of people. Treating me like a *child*. My mum would never do that.

'*I*'ve been,' said Sarah, smugly,

'Yes,' said Alice. 'You said.'

'*I* won't have to hold myself.'

'You wouldn't, anyway!' retorted Alice. 'You'd just pee in your pants!'

'I would not!' screeched Sarah.

Alice opened her mouth to shriek back, but her mum got in first.

'Alice, just leave your sister alone.'

'I'm not *touching* her,' said Alice.

'Well, don't. Duffy, I wonder,' said Alice's mum, 'would you mind if I asked you to sit between them?

Norman can't concentrate on his driving if they're carrying on like that. Alice! Change places.'

With a loud scoffing noise Alice slid across me to the other side. I shuffled myself further along the seat towards Sarah. I felt like I was in a war zone, wedged between the two of them. Like any minute the missiles might start flying.

'That's better,' said Alice's mum.

Her dad got into the car. 'Going for lift-off! Ten, nine, eight . . .'

The two girls joined in: 'Seven, six, five . . .'

It was kind of childish, but I thought maybe it was for Sarah's benefit. She was definitely on the slow side. Alice wasn't slow! She was sharp as a razor. But I'd already noticed, when her dad was around she had this tendency to get all little and girly. It really didn't suit her; her personality was far too spiky. But I guessed it was some sort of competitive thing. Vying with Sarah for her dad's attention. I could understand it, if she'd been adopted. Specially if she'd been adopted second. I wasn't passing judgement, or anything. I just found it a bit – well! A bit – cringe-making, I guess.

On the other hand, this was maybe how normal families behaved. A mum and dad, taking the kids out for the day. How would I know? My family's not like that. It never has been. I couldn't ever remember going anywhere with Mum and Dad and Charlotte, the four of us together. Charlotte had always been poorly, and before that there was me and my twitches. Dad really couldn't cope with my twitches. Alice's dad didn't seem to mind.

'Sing!' he roared. '*Old McDonald had a farm—*'

'*Ee aye ee aye oh!*'

I joined in, along with everyone else. My voice isn't what you would call tuneful, but then neither were Sarah's or Alice's. Not that it mattered. We couldn't be heard, anyway! The big bass booming of Alice's dad totally drowned out the uncertain pipings and warblings of the rest of us.

'Our dad's in the choir,' said Alice, proudly.

We drove for over three hours without stopping. Pretty relentless! For myself I didn't mind as I quite like driving. Mum hates it. She never drives anywhere if she can help it, so for me it was a bit of a treat, but after the first hour I noticed that Sarah went very quiet and Alice started huffing and puffing and wriggling on her seat, so that I wondered if she had made a mistake after all and was having to hold herself. Every time she huffed or puffed her mum would give her a warning glance.

'I'm just sick of *driving*,' she muttered.

Even I was starting to have had enough by the time we finally came to a halt.

'Where are we?' I said. We'd been driving so long I'd lost track.

'Does it matter?' said Alice.

I would have thought it did; but maybe not.

Sarah was clamouring to know when we were going to eat.

'Are we going to eat *now*, Dad? Are we going to eat now?'

'That is the general idea,' said her dad. 'Are you hungry, young master Duffy?'

I had to admit that I was.

'Then let us go and seek refreshment.'

We were in some village I'd never heard of. Tame-in-Arden. 'Bard country', according to Alice's dad.

'He means it's near Stratford on Avon,' said Alice.

I would have quite liked to see Stratford-upon-Avon, but I thought probably they had already been there, on some other trip. There didn't seem anything particularly special to see in Tame. Just a long street full of expensive-looking antique shops and art-and-craft boutiques, plus an old church with a churchyard.

'Oh, look!' cried Sarah, as we passed the church. 'Look at all the lovely graves!'

It was the most enthusiastic she'd been all morning.

'She likes graves,' said Alice.

'Dad!' Sarah hung on her dad's arm. 'Can we go and look at them? At the graves, Dad?'

'Afterwards,' said her dad. 'I have a hungry young man here, waiting to be fed.'

We sat in the garden of a pub and in defiance of Mum I drank Coke and hoped it wouldn't make me twitch. We all ate Scotch eggs and crisps, then Sarah demanded tiramisu. Alice's mum, in worried tones, said, 'I hope you don't regret that, Sarah.' It struck me that Alice's mum did a *lot* of worrying. I really didn't see what she had to worry about. Not compared with my mum.

After lunch we visited antique shops looking for a brass coal scuttle. Alice said they always looked for brass coal scuttles. Her dad had taken a fancy to have one, so now, whenever they went on magical mystery tours, that was what they ended up doing. Looking for coal scuttles.

'I expect when he's found one we'll start on something else,' said Alice.

When all the antique shops had been combed, without a single coal scuttle turning up, we went into the churchyard. Sarah became quite animated and went running from grave to grave, exclaiming over the headstones or the flowers.

'Oh, look, Dad! Someone's left these *beautiful* violets! Oh, look, oh, look! This person was only fourteen! Isn't that sad? Dad, isn't that sad?'

'She's so morbid,' said Alice.

Alice wanted to look in a bookshop she'd seen, but her mum said we didn't have time for that.

'We've got to get back. Duffy's gran will be worried if we don't get back.'

'But we haven't *done* anything!' said Alice.

Her mum said, 'What do you mean, we haven't done anything? Your dad's driven you almost a hundred miles!'

In spite of not having done anything, we were all quite tired on the way home. Alice and Sarah started quarrelling, in a whiny sort of way, without much heart in it. Their mum told them sharply to stop it.

'Your father's had a hard day! He doesn't need that.'

'It was her fault,' said Sarah.

'It's always my fault,' said Alice.

'Yes, it is,' said her mum. 'Just let your sister alone.'

Alice subsided, muttering. Sarah then announced that she felt sick.

'That's because you ate all that tiramisu,' said her mum. 'I warned you!'

I glanced at her, nervously. She was starting to look decidedly green.

'Mum, I'm going to throw up!'

'Well, I'm sorry, we can't stop,' said her mum.

I didn't see why not. It was all very well for her mum! She wasn't sitting next to her.

Alice's dad bellowed, 'Sing! Sing! It's all in the mind!'

Sarah opened her mouth – and was promptly sick all over the car.

'This is so gross,' said Alice.

I had to agree with her. Surely now we would stop?

'Ugh! Poo! The *stink*,' said Alice.

Her mum said, 'Alice!'

'Well, but it's disgusting,' said Alice.

Her mum leaned over the back of the seat and handed Sarah a packet of tissues.

'Mop yourself up. Then open the window and get some air.'

'Yes,' said Alice, 'and just *lean out* if you're going to do it again!'

On the whole it was quite a relief when we arrived back home. Alice's dad, without a word, went indoors. Alice's mum, in her flustery way, said, 'I'm so sorry,

Duffy! I hope that didn't ruin things for you. We did so want you to enjoy yourself! But Alice's dad doesn't like having to stop.'

I said that was OK. I said that I had enjoyed myself, it had been a really good day. I sort of meant it. I'd enjoyed the driving, and the singing. *And* the lunch (which hadn't brought on any extra twitches). I guess what I'd enjoyed above all was being part of a family – even if one of them had gone and thrown up.

'We'll do it again,' said Alice's mum. 'I'm afraid you'll have to excuse me now, I must see to Sarah!'

Alice's mum went flying indoors. Sarah had already gone in. It was just me and Alice.

'Did you really enjoy it?' said Alice.

I said, 'Yeah, it was great!'

'Are you being honest?'

I said, 'Yes. I am!'

That seemed to relax her. 'Dad wanted you to have a good time,' she said.

'I did have a g-good time!'

'He's a brilliant driver,' said Alice, 'isn't he?'

I agreed that he was.

'But it was pretty pukey in there at the end! Sarah's always throwing up. She gets car sick, even when she takes pills. It's her own fault, she shouldn't have stuffed herself with pudding. Now she'll have to clean it up,' said Alice, in tones of satisfaction, as Sarah came trailing out of the house with a bucket. 'Serve her right! She could at least have done it out the window.'

Over tea, Nan was eager to hear all the details. Where we'd been, what we'd done. I said that we'd driven almost a hundred miles to a place called Tame-in-Arden to look for a brass coal scuttle.

'That'll be Norman,' said Nan. 'He gets these enthusiasms!'

'Yeah, w-well, we didn't find one,' I said. I added that it seemed a long way to go, just for a coal scuttle.

'Get away with you!' said Nan. 'You enjoyed the drive, didn't you?'

'I did,' I said. 'S-Sarah didn't. She got sick and threw up all over the car.'

'Poor little soul,' said Nan. 'I always feel so sorry for Sarah! She's such a sad little thing. I dread to think what would have become of her if Norman hadn't taken her on.'

'Her mum made her clear it up,' I said. 'When we got back . . . she made her go out with a b-bucket and clear it up.'

'That's not right,' said Nan. 'It's hardly her fault if she gets sick. But the mum's a weird one! It has to be said. Between you and me—' she lowered her voice '— I often wonder what he saw in her.'

I'd wondered that, too. Alice's dad was so big, and warm, and outgoing, with this really great sense of humour. Her mum was like a wisp. Like a shadow. Hardly there. And fretting all the time! And I didn't think it was fair to make Sarah go and mop up her sick. *Or* to make us all sit there in the middle of it. We could easily have just stopped the car for five minutes to clean it up.

I said this to Nan, who agreed with me.

'It's not right, embarrassing a child like that. I'm surprised Norman didn't say something.'

'He doesn't like stopping,' I said.

'What do you mean, he doesn't like stopping?'

'Alice's mum said . . . he doesn't like stopping.'

'Rubbish! What nonsense!'

'It's what she said.'

'More like she just wanted to get back.'

'I don't think they do what she wants,' I said. 'She's not head of the household.'

'She's the mother,' said Nan. 'It's up to her.'

The way Nan said it was like, that's that: end of conversation. She wouldn't hear anything against Big Norm. Not that I'd really been saying anything against him. It was more against Alice's mum. I just felt she ought to stick up for the girls a bit more than she did; that was all.

Later in the evening, while Nan was watching television, I wandered out into the garden. It was still quite light, and I could see a figure perched on the wall.

'Hi,' said Alice. 'It's me.'

'I'm s-supposed to be going to b-bed,' I said. 'But it's too hot. I didn't w-want to.'

'I never want to,' said Alice. 'I hate going to bed.'

I said, 'What, always?'

'Yes,' said Alice. '*Always*.'

There was a pause.

'I quite like it in winter,' I said. 'I like to curl up under the d-duvet and pretend I'm in a s-s-s-s-*sleeping* bag at the North Pole.'

'I don't like it any time,' said Alice. 'What's to like about it?'

'Well . . .' How could I explain? Being in bed was like being in a nest. It was like being *safe*.

'Safe from what?' said Alice, when I told her.

I said, 'Things that are out to g-get you!'

Wild animals. Frostbite. People who laugh at you behind your back.

Alice tossed her head. 'If things are out to *get you*,' she said, 'they'll *get you* wherever you are.' She sprang down, into her own garden. 'Life's not a fairy story, Oddball!'

Whoever said it was?

5

Sunday morning, Nan went to church. I felt she would have liked me to go with her, but being Nan she would never ask. You have to respect other people's beliefs, is what she says. 'It doesn't do to push things down a person's throat.'

I'd discussed it with Mum before she went off to America. Mum had said only to go if I wanted to.

'Don't feel that you have to. Nan won't be offended.'

I couldn't make up my mind. There was one part of me that felt I ought to – I mean, it seemed only polite, when I was staying in Nan's house. On the other hand, I'm never absolutely certain that I believe in any of it, so surely it would be hypocritical?

Nan could obviously see that I was hesitating.

'Don't feel under any pressure,' she said. 'I'd be delighted if you came, but not because you feel you have to. Only if you really want.'

'M-maybe n-next time,' I said.

'That's all right,' said Nan. 'I'm not hassling you.'

It's this really big thing in Nan's life. It happened after my granddad died. She and Granddad were pretty close, so I suppose she needed something to kind of . . . fill the gap. I don't quite mean it like that! I know it brings her comfort. It's just that I can't seem to get into it, personally speaking. You have to have faith. But how do you get it? This is what no one can ever explain.

After Nan had left I went out into the garden to look for Alice. She seemed to spend her life sitting on the wall, but this morning she wasn't there. Too late, I remembered that she'd said how she still had to go to church even though she was a heathen.

I wished for a minute that I'd gone with Nan after all; at least I would have seen Alice. We could have sat and been heathens together. If I *was* a heathen. Sometimes I think I might be, then at other times I waver. Mostly I just feel undecided. Because, I mean, how can you possibly know? Anyway, going to church just to see Alice would be every bit as hypocritical as going to church to be polite. Alice only went because she had to. Because her dad was the big cheese and sang in the choir.

I decided that I would go back indoors and spend the morning on the computer, instead. Nan could hardly complain about me hunching. If I'd been at home I would have been on it all day, every day. I reckoned she ought to be grateful to Alice, keeping me away from it as much as she did.

At lunch time, when Nan returned, she suggested we went off in the car to visit some gardens she fancied seeing.

'Make a nice outing,' she said.

I'm not really into gardens, to be honest, but it was obviously something Nan was keen on so I gave this little grunt to signify enthusiasm and said, 'Could Alice c-come with us, do you think?'

I knew she wasn't Nan's favourite person, but I'd been out with Alice and her mum and dad so it seemed only fair she could come out with me and Nan. Nan, however, said that Alice wouldn't be allowed to, on a Sunday.

'Norman's very strict. The rest of the week they have all the freedom they could want. Too much in her case, if you ask me. She only abuses it. But Sundays are special, they're a family day. Norman's a very religious man,' said Nan. 'Very spiritual. He thought of being a priest at one time. He could have been. But then he felt his mission lay elsewhere.'

'So they all have to s-stay in?' I said. 'All Sunday?'

'And why not?' Nan bristled. She'd really got it bad! The hero worship thing, I mean.

'It seems a b-bit extr-reme,' I said.

'Not at all! I think it's good there should be one day in the week that's different.'

'Yeah, but it's h-hard on Alice,' I said, 'if she doesn't b-believe in any of it.'

Nan sniffed. 'No, well, she wouldn't. She'd do anything just to be perverse.'

Nan had really got it in for Alice. I guessed in her case it was this thing she had about Big Norm, him being the Great I Am and Nan reckoning Alice gave him a load of grief. But it wasn't just Nan! Everyone seemed to have it in for Alice. Her mum, her gran, her sister. They couldn't all have a thing about Big Norm. *Could* they?

Maybe they could. And maybe it was true. Maybe Alice did give him a load of grief. Even though I was her friend, I could see she mightn't be the easiest person to live with. But I wasn't sure her dad would be all that easy, either. I mean, he was fun, and I liked him, but he could be a bit . . . well! Swamping.

'She's really got you wrapped round her little finger, hasn't she?' said Nan. 'I knew she would! I warned you. She's a manipulative little so-and-so.'

'D-doesn't seem to have m-manipulated you,' I said.

'No, and she won't! I know too much about her. I wonder if Steven would like to come with us? I should have asked him. I'll give them a go! See if he'd like to.'

I waited with foreboding while Nan went into the hall to ring. Fortunately, there was no reply. Nan was disappointed; she seemed to think it would have been nice for me.

'Now you'll be stuck on your own with a boring old woman!'

'You're not boring,' I said.

'Oh, no?' said Nan. 'Just pull the other one! I'm perfectly well aware you'd rather stay hunched over that thing up there. But you've been on it all morning! It's time you got out and saw the world a bit.'

I resigned myself: there are some things you just can't fight. At any rate it was less fraught being on my own with Nan than having a resentful Steven trailing round with us. That would have been totally *excruciating*. Both for him and for me. But I did wish Alice could have come! I found that I missed her. I missed the way she called me Oddball and giggled at me and took me off – 'D-d-d-d-' – and finished my sentences for me when I got stuck. Other people don't do that; they're too embarrassed. They just try to pretend it's not happening, which then embarrasses me as well. Nan would probably have said Alice was rude and tactless, but then Nan never had a good word to say for her anyway.

Later that day, in the evening, I wandered up the garden again, just in case.

'Alice?'

I hoisted myself up the wall and peered over.

'She's not here.' Sarah was in the garden, bouncing a ball and swatting at it with a tennis racquet. 'She's in her room. She's in disgrace.'

'W-why?' I said. 'What's she d-d-d—'

Sarah stood waiting.

'DONE!' I shouted, and shot out an arm.

'She's been rude,' said Sarah. She said it in these tones of gloating satisfaction. 'She yelled at Mum, so Mum told her to go to her room and stay there. She won't be let out till Dad gets home. Maybe not even then. She might have to stay there all night.'

I looked up at the house. Alice's bedroom window was open. If I shouted, would she hear me? But what would I shout?

'Alice-it's-Duffy! I'm-sorry-you-re-in-trouble!'

Except that it probably wouldn't come out that way. I probably wouldn't get any further than 'Alice-it's-Oddb-b-b—'

Sarah was studying me from under her fringe. She had this fringe of lank hair that fell over her eyes. I got the feeling she wasn't embarrassed by what Dad used to call my *antics* any more than Alice was. But Alice was my friend. Sarah treated me like I was some kind of weird insect in a specimen dish. She forked her fringe aside with a finger.

'You can't speak to her,' she said. 'She's not allowed.'

There was something about Sarah that made me cringe. Not because she was childish, or because she was slow. Because she was *malicious*. She really liked it that Alice was in trouble. She was relishing it. She was *gloating*.

'This is what happens,' said Sarah, 'when people are *bad* . . . they get punished.' She tossed her ball into the air and swatted at it. 'She's bad all of the time. That's why you can't see her.'

'That's all right,' I said. 'I'll c-catch her tomorrow.'

I slid down off the wall and slowly walked back up the garden. I realized, when I went to bed that night, that I could see Alice's window from mine. I remembered her saying how she hated going to bed – and now she was shut in her room right round till morning. It seemed a bit harsh. She must have said something really bad. *She's bad all of the time.* But that was Sarah. You couldn't rely on what Sarah said.

I reckoned Alice and her mum had probably just had a bit of a row, like girls do with their mums. Me and Mum never row, but I might well have done with Dad, if he'd stuck around. In the past I'd always felt too lowly and insignificant, what with having Tourette's and putting him to shame, but some of the things he said to Mum, before he left . . . he made her cry. I didn't like that. It got me really mad. So if he'd stayed, it might just have been me shut in my room all night.

Or maybe not, 'cos I don't think Mum would have let him. Mum always stuck up for me. Whenever Dad got impatient at my twitching, she'd tell him to back off. Alice's mum didn't seem to stick up for her at all. Nobody seemed to stick up for Alice.

In the morning there was another e-mail from Auntie Marje.

Dear Both,
Charlotte's op is at 2pm. Our time. I will let you know as soon as it's over. Keep faith! Love from Marje.

Two pm California time. That would make it . . . I counted forward on my fingers. Ten o'clock! At ten o'clock this evening they would be giving Charlotte an anaesthetic to make her sleep. They would be wheeling her into the operating theatre on a trolley. They would be taking out their scalpels—

I felt this lump, like a cricket ball, rise into my throat. I didn't want to think about it! Charlotte was so little.

She was so innocent, and so helpless! Far too young to know why they were doing these terrible things to her. Cutting her open. Taking bits out. Putting bits in. How could you understand, at only three years old?

I turned, and galloped down the stairs, out of the house, into the garden. 'Alice?'

I swung myself up on to the wall. Where was she? She had to be there! They couldn't keep her shut in her room all night and all morning.

'*Alice!*'

I shouted it out, but the garden was silent and empty. Then something caught my eye. Something blue, down in the undergrowth. Alice's T shirt! She was in her hole. In her time warp. What was it she had said? *Different plane of existence.*

I jumped down off the wall, fell on to all fours and crawled through the bushes and the brambles to the old fox earth. Alice was there, curled up in a tight ball, knees hugged to chin, just the way she had shown me.

'Alice?' I whispered. 'It's Oddb-ball.'

No response. She was on her different plane of existence. Couldn't hear me.

'*Alice!*' I reached out a hand and dabbed at her. I'm not very good at the touching thing; it tends to embarrass me. Except if it's Charlotte. Anyone else tries to hug or kiss me, I shy away. Even if it's Mum or Nan.

Alice didn't shy away. She didn't flinch, she didn't shrink. It was like she didn't even feel me.

'Alice, p-please!' I whispered.

I crouched next to her, curling myself up, knees to chin, the same as she was. For the longest time, neither of us moved or spoke. Then, without lifting her head, Alice muttered, 'What d'you want?'

'Just w-wanted some c-company,' I whispered.

'What for?'

'Just f-felt a bit l-lonely.'

'Why?'

'Just d-did.'

Alice made a noise that sounded like 'Hump!'. But at least she didn't tell me to go away, or that she was on a different plane of existence.

'Had an e-mail,' I said. 'From Am-merica.'

Alice grunted.

'It's t-ten o'c-clock. T-t-t—' My arm shot out. 'Tonight!'

For the first time, Alice raised her head. She looked at me. 'What is?'

'The operation!'

'On Charlotte?'

'Yes. I'm s-scared!' I said. I wouldn't have admitted it to anyone but Alice. Not even to Nan. 'She's so l-little! It's not f-f-f-f—'

'Fair,' said Alice. 'Life isn't. I told you, didn't I? It's a lie, about God. There isn't any God.'

I wasn't quite ready to accept that.

'We d-don't know for sure,' I said.

'I do,' said Alice.

'How c-can you? How c-can anyone?'

68

'Some kind of God it is, then,' said Alice. 'Letting little kids suffer!'

That was true. Nobody in their right mind could say that Charlotte deserved what was happening to her. She was too young! She hadn't ever done anything bad in her three years. She'd been sick since the day she was born.

It still seemed a big step to wipe God out completely.

'Your d-dad believes in Him,' I said. 'I mean, Her,' I added, in case Alice was a feminist. She probably was.

Alice just snorted. 'Him, Her! Where's the difference? Whichever it is, it'd have to be a pretty sick sort of God, if you ask me.'

'But if s-someone like your dad,' I said.

'What's that supposed to mean?' She turned on me. 'Someone like my dad?'

'S-someone g-*good*,' I said.

'You don't have to believe in God to be good,' said Alice. 'And what *is* good, anyway?'

I wanted to say, 'Your dad!' I wanted to tell her how much I would have liked to have a dad like that. Especially now, with all that was happening to Charlotte. A dad who'd be there for you. A dad you could feel safe with. But it would have sounded too pathetic, so I didn't.

'Tell me about yours,' said Alice.

'My d-dad?'

'Yes. Tell me about him!'

'N-nothing to tell.'

'There's got to be *something*. Why did he leave home?'

' 'Cos of me.'

Alice's eyes widened. ' 'Cos of *you*?'

I explained how Dad had always been ashamed of me. How he hadn't liked people knowing I was his son. How he hadn't wanted Mum to have any more babies in case they turned out like me.

'But I th-think Mum wanted one that was normal.'

It is what I have always believed. I have always believed that Mum secretly hoped, if she had one that was normal, it would make things all right again between her and Dad. But then Charlotte was born, and was poorly, and Dad told Mum that he couldn't take any more of it, it was wearing him down. 'He'd p-put up with m-me all these years—'

'He said *that*?' said Alice.

'He didn't know I w-was listening.'

Alice pulled a strand of hair round to her mouth. She munched on it a while.

'Did you love him?' she said, at last.

I nodded.

'Even after what he said?'

'He was my d-dad,' I said.

'Did you miss him when he left?'

'I – g-guess so.'

I must have done. Surely? It was difficult to remember. From the moment Dad left us, our lives had been turned upside down. We'd sold the house. Moved into a flat. Dumped half our stuff, 'cos there wasn't any room for it. I'd become a computer freak. I'd got computers like Nan had got religion. Mum had gone into overdrive, raising money for Charlotte's operation. There'd been Mum speaking on the radio, Mum addressing meetings, Mum in the local paper. Photographs. Questions. And finally, the cheques coming in. Cheques arriving by every post. Cheques for a fiver, cheques for five hundred. Mum in tears, but of happiness, this time. Overwhelmed by people's kindness. Looking back, there hadn't really been much opportunity for missing Dad.

'What about your mum?' said Alice. 'How does she manage, on her own?'

'She manages OK,' I said. Mum had turned into quite a managing sort of person.

'But what about paying the bills? And getting the car serviced? And checking the bank statements? Who does all that if your dad isn't there?'

I said, 'M-Mum does.'

Alice was studying me, searchingly, her blue eyes fixed on mine.

'Didn't she go all to pieces?'

'N-no. Not really.' I thought perhaps for Mum it had been almost a relief. Dad had made her cry so many times since Charlotte was born.

I said this to Alice, and she shook her head, as if she were having difficulty believing me. I could see why. She was obviously thinking of *her* mum – who was pretty feeble in comparison with mine. I could imagine that Alice's mum might well go to pieces.

'I looked for you last night,' I said, 'but you w-weren't here.'

'No,' said Alice. 'I was up in my room. I was there all evening. But I didn't mind! It didn't bother me one little bit. I didn't want to be downstairs with them, anyway. I'm busy,' she said. 'I'm writing a book.'

I said, 'A b-*book*?'

'It's going to be called *Malice in Blunderland*.'

'Oh! Hey! I get it,' I said. 'That's clever!'

'You could read it, if you like. D'you want to? I could let you see just bits of it. But if I do,' said Alice, 'you mustn't ever talk about it to anyone. Do you understand? I mean it! You mustn't ever, *ever*, say anything. 'Cos if you do . . .'

'I wouldn't,' I said.

'It might mean I have to kill myself,' said Alice.

She paused a moment, to let it sink in.

'You are the only person in the entire living breathing universe that I will ever have shown it to. The only person I have ever even *mentioned* it to.'

A row of prickles went shivering down my spine. I felt honoured; but also a bit nervous. It sounded like rather a lot of responsibility.

'Course, you don't have to if you don't want to,' said Alice.

I wasn't sure that I did; I found her intensity a bit scary. Suppose I read the thing and hated it? Or just thought it was drivel? What happened then?

'Well, do you?' said Alice. 'Or don't you?'

'Um . . . y-yes,' I said. 'Course I do!'

'I'll bring it round,' she said. 'Later. I can't go and get

it right now 'cos it's in my bedroom. It's hidden away to keep it from *her*. But I don't feel like going indoors just yet, so I'll bring it in a little while. OK?'

'Mm!' I smiled, brightly. 'I'm s-sorry if I disturbed you while you were on another plane,' I said.

'That's all right,' said Alice. 'I don't mind *you* disturbing me. You're on the same plane with me. We're on it together, just the two of us. We're both Oddballs.'

'Knickers!' I cried, shooting out an arm. But she wouldn't play.

'It's only because of that,' she said, 'that I'm letting you read my secrets. Because we're on the same plane of existence and I know that I can trust you.'

6

I spent the rest of the morning on the computer. So long as I was with Alice I was OK; but without her I was starting to feel definite withdrawal symptoms. Nan always says that when you read books you find yourself transported to another world. She can never understand how I can be transported by a mere *computer*.

'A machine! That's all it is . . . a machine!'

She thinks when I'm sitting there I'm just playing games; just being mindless. I've tried to explain it to her. How you can almost become one with the computer. How you can go on these endless journeys into realms far beyond anything you could possibly imagine, where time and space and everything ordinary simply cease to exist. I've tried to tell her, but she just shakes her head, as if to say, *what nonsense he talks!* Maybe she's too old. Or maybe she just doesn't have the right sort of brain. Not everybody does.

When I really become merged, when me and the machine become one entity, so to speak, I sometimes find it quite difficult to bring myself back again. To be on the safe side I set my alarm for one o'clock, which was about the time Nan's car usually turned into the drive. I was waiting for her as she came through the door, but she still guessed where I'd been.

'Upstairs! Hunched! Or were you with that Alice?'

I couldn't decide which she thought was worse.

'Poor Alice,' I said.

'Poor Alice?' said Nan. 'What's poor about her, I'd like to know? If anyone's fallen on her feet, she has. Doesn't know when she's well off, that's her trouble. Now! Listen. There's an exhibition on at the Central Library. Egyptian mummies. How about we go along after lunch? Have a look round, get a cup of tea . . . what do you reckon?'

I hadn't known Nan was interested in Egyptian mummies, and I didn't think, really, that she was; but she seemed to feel the need to lay on some entertainment so I agreed that it sounded like fun. I didn't bother asking whether we could take Alice. I'd gone down the garden and looked over the wall, and she was still crouched at the entrance to her hole, so I thought she probably wouldn't thank me for disturbing her. In any case, I knew what Nan's answer would be.

I couldn't help wondering, though, how long Alice planned on staying. She'd been there all morning. Did she do this often? Or only when she was upset? I found it a bit disturbing, but I didn't say anything. To Nan, I mean. I didn't want to produce another tirade.

Nan was pretty beat when we got back from the museum. We'd walked all round the exhibition, had a cup of tea in the library tea shop, and then gone on to

75

the shopping centre and walked round there, as well. Not looking for anything special, as far as I could make out, but just killing time.

'We don't want to brood,' said Nan, sinking down at the kitchen table. She didn't have to say what it was we didn't want to brood about. My first thought every morning when I woke up was for Charlotte; she was in my mind every night when I went to bed, as well. I guessed it must be the same for Nan.

'I doubt we'll hear anything before morning,' she said.

I protested that Auntie Marje had promised to let us know straight away, as soon as the operation was over, but as Nan pointed out, it wasn't going to be over in five minutes.

'Could take a few hours . . . it's not like just whipping an appendix out.'

I didn't want to think about it. I just wanted it to be over.

'So! What shall we do this evening?' said Nan. 'Are you going to stay downstairs and keep me company?'

I knew that I would have to. Nan was every bit as anxious as I was, it wouldn't be fair to leave her on her own.

'I'll have a look what's on the telly,' she said.

As Nan reached out for the paper, there was a loud rat-a-tat at the front door. Rat tatta tat tat, tat *tat*.

Nan said, 'Who's that, battering the house down? Go and have a look, there's a good boy! Save my poor legs.'

Who it was, was Alice. Even as I opened the door her hand was raised to start battering again.

'I like door knockers!' she said.

'Yes, we h-heard,' I said.

'Well, it's what they're for, isn't it?' said Alice. 'No point if you don't knock with them. Here!' She thrust a Jiffy bag at me. 'I've brought you my story. What I've done of it, so far. But you've got to remember what you promised!'

'Not to tell anyone,' I said.

'Right. I mean it! See you tomorrow. Oh!' She turned at the front gate. 'There's the books in there, as well. The ones I said you could borrow. You don't have to read them immediately, but until you've read them you won't properly appreciate my story. OK?'

I nodded. 'OK!'

Alice flapped a hand and disappeared. I went back to the kitchen with the Jiffy bag. 'What's that you've got?' said Nan.

'Just s-something Alice gave me. Something she wants me to r-read.'

Nan was eyeing the Jiffy bag suspiciously. As if there might be a bomb in there. Or a load of porn. I upended it and shook out two old-fashioned, musty-looking books and a wodge of typed pages held together with a rusty jumbo clip.

'Well, now! Will you look at that?' said Nan, reaching for the books. '*Alice in Wonderland* . . . *Alice Through the Looking Glass.*'

I couldn't work out whether she approved of Alice's taste or was secretly disappointed it wasn't something she could complain about.

'What's that lot?' said Nan.

'A story she's written. But it's p-private,' I said, snatching it up.

I read Alice's story while Nan watched *EastEnders* and *Survivor* and *Soap Secrets*. I have to admit, I got quite engrossed in it. It was definitely weird, and also, in places, a bit creepy. To be honest, I wasn't really sure that I understood any of it, but I might have known Alice wouldn't write anything ordinary. She wouldn't write the sort of stuff that girls normally write. Well, the girls in my class at school, who are the only girls I know anything about. Mr Hart sometimes reads their stories out loud, much to the girls' embarrassment. They're always about going on holiday, meeting gorgeous guys and falling in love. The girls who've written them always blush furiously, while the boys all snigger.

Alice's story was quite different. If anyone had asked me what it was about, I wouldn't really have been able to tell them. But I kept on reading, all the same.

Alice's story.

MALICE IN BLUNDERLAND

I

Alice was having a dream. She was in a picture frame, hanging on her bedroom wall. A white rabbit, dressed in a check coat and carrying a watch, had just scurried past her. In a corner sat a sheep, doing some knitting. The sheep was pale and fluffy, with glasses on its nose. Its knitting was a long string, full of holes, like a dish rag.

'Slip one, slop one,' bleated the sheep, as it knitted.

Alice stared as the rabbit consulted his watch, then shook his head as if vexed about something and scampered off down a nearby rabbit hole.

'How very odd!' thought Alice.

The sheep just went on knitting, slipping and slopping and dropping its stitches.

Suddenly, from the left-hand corner of the picture, there was a great commotion. A swirl of dust, and the blare of what sounded like a thousand trumpets, and a Red Queen burst upon the scene. She was going very fast and shouting at the top of her voice.

'Little girl, where are you? Ah, there you are! I have been looking for you all over. Come! Give me your hand. Let us away!'

'Away to where?' gasped Alice.

'Never mind where! No time to lose!' The Red Queen flew across the picture, dragging Alice with her. 'I have a game for you to play!'

'I am not sure that I want to play a game,' said Alice, snatching back her hand (which the Queen had in a firm grasp). 'I would rather stay here, if it is all the same to you. Your Majesty,' she added, for fear of being thought rude.

'It is not all the same,' snapped the Queen. 'The Other One is not available and I am having to make do with you!'

Other One? thought Alice, bewildered. Which 'Other One' is she talking about?

'I am afraid,' said Alice, 'that I don't quite follow you. Your Majesty.'

'I am talking of the other little girl! The one who usually plays with me. You are very much second best but you will have to do. Come along, now! Be quick!'

'But I don't wish to come!' cried Alice.

'It is not a question of what you wish. Just do as you're told!'

'You really must learn,' bleated the sheep, 'to be a bit more grateful.'

'Grateful for what?' spluttered Alice.

'Grateful for all that has been done for you!' And the sheep, in its agitation, dropped a whole flurry of stitches.

'Make haste, make haste!' The Queen had Alice in her grasp again. Her fingers dug into Alice's arm. 'I do not have all day!'

'But you haven't told me where we are going,' protested Alice.

'It is not your place to ask questions!' snapped the Queen. 'I am the one who decides. Now, get a move on!'

'I won't!' cried Alice. She dug her heels in. She could be quite stubborn on occasion. 'I'm not playing any games, and you can't make me!'

The sheep gave a frightened bleat and dropped all the rest of its stitches.

'Ingratitude!' shrilled a Duchess, who had just somehow managed to get into the picture. (Where had SHE come from? wondered Alice.) 'This is disgraceful! Have you no regard for rank? This is royalty you're speaking to!'

'I'm very sorry, I'm sure,' said Alice, sinking down into a curtsey (as best she could, with the Red Queen still hanging on *to her.) 'But I don't see why I should have to go and play a game I don't want to play just because she is a queen and I am a nobody!'*

'Yes, you are!' screeched the Duchess, hitting Alice over the head with a soup ladle. 'At least you recognize the fact! Just remember it in future and act accordingly.'

'I'm doing the best I can,' said Alice, wobbling up out of her curtsey.

'Not good enough, not good enough!' The Duchess aimed another smack at Alice with her ladle.

'Ouch!' cried Alice. 'You're hurting me!'

'Yes, and I shall hurt you some more if you don't learn to behave yourself,' said the Duchess.

Alice tore herself away and began to run as fast as she could to the far side of the picture. The Duchess and the Red Queen ran after her. The Duchess was old and slow but the Red Queen went like the wind. As she ran, she screamed at the top of her voice: 'Off with her knickers! Off with her knickers!'

Alice didn't like the sound of that at all. If this was the sort of game the Red Queen had in mind, she most certainly didn't want to play it. There was only one thing to be done.

'Thank goodness for rabbit holes!' thought Alice.

She was just small enough to squeeze down there. As she did so, she heard the Red Queen's voice, still shouting in the distance: 'Off with her Knickerssssssssss!'

('What are you laughing at?' said Nan.

'N-nothing,' I said. 'Just s-something I read.')

Alice shivered. This really was a most unpleasant dream! She would be glad when she woke up.

II

Alice still seemed to be dreaming, though she was no longer down the rabbit hole. She wasn't quite sure where she was. A White Queen sat on a cushion, doing some knitting. She had a crown on her head (which was how Alice knew she was a queen) and glasses on her nose. She looked rather pale and woolly; not nearly as threatening as the Red Queen. At least, thought Alice, this one is not racing about and trying to take off my knickers.

'You were saying,' said the Queen, in a weary sort of voice.

'Was I?' said Alice.

'So you said. Of course it is impossible to be sure. It is next to impossible to believe a word you say. But you did say it,' said the Queen, peering through her glasses at a row of stitches.

'In that case,' said Alice, 'perhaps I should continue.'

'If you must,' said the Queen. 'But be warned! I want none of your nonsense.'

Indeed, no, thought Alice. We do not want nonsense. She remembered, now: she had been about to do a recitation.

Alice took up her position, in the middle of the room. (She supposed it was a room, though it had no doors or windows.)

'Recitation,' she said.

> *'Come into my parlour, said the spider to the fly.*
> *I'll teach you how, and wherefore,*
> *And which, and what, and why*
> *The sky is blue, the grass is green,*
> *And children as a general rule,*

> *Both at home, and at school,*
> *Must be content with being seen.*
> *Not strive to make themselves be heard,*
> *By shrieking out with tales of woe,*
> *And wicked lies that are not so,*
> *And many a malicious word.*
> *Children should be seen, not heard . . .'*

'And that, you know,' said Alice, sadly, 'would appear to be the general shape of things.'

'And a very good shape it is, too,' said the Queen. 'Let it be a lesson to you. Such rubbish as you talk! It is not at all seemly.'

'Things certainly are not always what they seem,' agreed Alice.

The Queen clicked impatiently with her knitting needles.

'I have no idea to which THINGS you are referring. Be more specific, if you please!'

'Well, I will be,' said Alice, 'if that is what you really want. But then again, if it isn't, it isn't. Which is what I suspect.'

'You suspect too much altogether,' said the Queen. 'I wish you would just be quiet! I have had enough for one day.'

'I have had enough for every day,' muttered Alice. 'Not that anyone is interested.'

'How can you expect them to be so,' said the Queen, 'when you will persist in telling lies? Slip one, slop one. Now look what you have made me do!'

The Queen, becoming agitated, dropped a whole row of stitches and threw up her knitting in despair. Any minute now, thought Alice, and she will turn into a white sheep. Yes, there *she goes! Now she will start bleating at me.*

'Such ingratitude,' bleated the sheep, pushing its glasses further up its nose. 'Why can you not be seen and not heard, the same as other little girls?'

'I am not heard,' said Alice. 'That is the whole problem.'

'So what do you expect me to do about it?' The sheep picked up its knitting and regarded it, helplessly. It was all in a tangle, and full of holes. 'I do what I can, I cannot do more. That is a fact of life. We must all make the best of things. It would help,' cried the sheep, working itself into a froth, 'if you would stop inventing all these stories! How can I keep any stitches on my needle if you are constantly bombarding me with the sound of your voice? It is lies!' screeched the sheep. 'All lies! Oh, I shall go demented! You will be the death of me!'

And the sheep ran bleating up the chimney, leaving Alice quite on her own with no one to talk to.

Well, I tried, thought Alice. But what is the use if no one will listen?

The moral of this story reads
That no one cares for children's needs.

III

After the sheep flew up the chimney, Alice found herself in a clearing in some woods. The way one hops from place to place, thought Alice, is really most confusing. Now she seemed to be at some kind of party. A long table was set for tea. A Mad

Hatter sat there, together with a March Hare and a Dormouse fast asleep with its head in a teapot.

'Good afternoon,' said Alice.

'Well, if you say so,' said the Hatter. 'I must confess I hadn't noticed.'

'It's hard to be sure,' said Alice, 'the way things keep changing. But it seemed to be when I left.'

'Oh, so you've left, have you?' said the Hare. 'I suppose you've come to join us, instead?'

'Was she invited?' hissed the Hatter.

'Who knows?' said the Hare, rather glumly.

'Actually,' said Alice, 'I don't believe I was. At any rate, I have no memory of it. I think most probably,' she said, 'I'm just passing through.'

'That is all right, then.' The Hatter relaxed. 'I have no problem with you passing through. Just say what you have to say!'

Alice thought about it. 'I could tell you a story,' she said.

They liked that idea. 'We could do with a good story,' said the Hare.

'Just a short one, then,' said Alice. 'Then I really shall have to be on my way.'

This was Alice's story:

> 'Dearest Dear and Just Behave
> Were spoiling for a fight.
> They planned to fight from early morn
> And late into the night.

But then appeared a monstrous shape,
With claws as sharp as knives.
Which frightened both the children so,
They ran to save their lives.'

When Alice had finished, there was a long silence.

'That is it,' said Alice, hopefully.

'IT?' said the Hatter. 'How can it be?'

'It just is,' said Alice.

'But where did they run to?'

Alice hadn't given much thought to that. 'Does it matter?' she said.

'Well, yes,' said the Hatter, 'since you ask.'

'Do they escape?' said the Hare. 'That is what I want to know.'

'One would like to think so,' said Alice. 'But in my experience life is not like that.'

There was a pause, while they thought about it.

'Like what?' said the Hatter, at last.

'Happy endings,' said Alice.

'We certainly don't want an UNHAPPY one,' said the Hare.

'Well, I'm sorry,' said Alice, 'but there's nothing very much that I can do about it. It seems,' she said, sadly, 'to be inevitable.'

'Oh! Oh!' The Hare plucked the Dormouse out of the teapot and plunged it straight back in again. 'Now she is using long words!'

'Just go away.' The Hatter waved an impatient hand. 'We don't wish to hear your stories. Not if they have unhappy endings. There is enough unhappiness in the world without you adding to it. It is probably all lies, anyway. And take that dormouse out *of the teapot!' he added. 'Pour me another cup of tea!'*

Alice obediently removed the Dormouse and poured out the tea, then dejectedly wandered off among the trees. It seemed that no one wanted to hear her stories.

IV

Stranger and stranger, thought Alice. This looks as if it might be the beach at Brighton, except that I have never seen such odd-looking creatures before.

'Would you mind telling me,' she said, as politely as she could, 'what manner of creature you are?'

'I am a Mock Purple,' said one. 'And this, standing next to me, is a Purpose.'

'How very interesting!' said Alice.

'We think so,' agreed the Mock Purple.

'How about you?' said the Purpose. 'Are you of any interest?'

'That would probably depend,' said Alice, 'upon which way one looked at things.'

The Mock Purple said that they were looking the only way they knew how. 'Straight ahead for England, and over the sea to France. And while we are looking, we wait to be entertained.'

'Is that what you have come to do?' said the Purpose.

Alice supposed that it might be. At any rate, she could always try. I keep trying, she thought. One day someone will listen to me.

'Well?' said the Mock Purple. 'We're waiting!'

'Very well,' said Alice. She stood herself upon a rock and began:

87

' "Will you come a little closer?" hissed a Redding to a Child.
"Pray do not fear, but just come near! You'll find me very
mild.
"See how eagerly the Other One is waiting to advance!
Will you, won't you, will you, won't you,
Won't you join the dance?"

"You can really have no notion how delightful it will be
When you give in to my pleading and come and dance with
   me!"
But the Child replied, "Just go away!" and took a stubborn
stance.

Said she really was determined that she would not join the
dance.
Would not, could not, would not, could not,
Would not join the dance.

The Redding, he then turned on her, and snatched her 'gainst
her will.
"You'll do as I decree!" he cried. "Just stay there and keep still!
I asked you nicely, did I not? I gave you every chance!
Now will you, won't you, will you, won't you,
You'd BETTER join the dance!" '

'Oh, yawn!' said the Mock Purple, as Alice came to the end.
   'I am already half asleep,' said the Purpose.
   'Why could she not just join the dance and be done with it?'
   'Instead of making all that stupid amount of fuss?'

88

'It's all made up, anyway. We didn't want a MADE UP story,' said the Mock Purple. 'Anyone can just MAKE UP stories.'

'It's really no better,' said the Purpose, 'than telling outright lies.'

'Oh!' cried Alice. She scooped up a handful of sand and flung it at them. 'Go swim in the sea, you stupid creatures!'

'Well!' said Nan. 'You seem to be enjoying that, whatever it is.'

'It's good,' I said. 'I think it may be a bit like *Alice in Wonderland*.'

I am not totally ignorant. Even I had heard of the Mock Turtle, and the Mad Hatter's Tea Party.

'She'll have copied it,' said Nan.

I frowned. *Had* Alice copied it? I couldn't tell, not having read the books. It did seem suspiciously well written.

'She's like that,' said Nan. 'She'll claim to have done something – say something's happened – and it's obvious she's just made it up. Like she'll tell you she's written something, and all she'll have done is just take it out of a book. She's a very strange child.'

People think I'm pretty strange. But what people think isn't necessarily true.

'You don't want to believe everything she tells you,' said Nan. 'It's not her fault; I'm not saying it is. She had a bad start in life. In and out of children's homes . . . her natural mother was a junkie.' Nan spat the word, distastefully, as if it might contaminate her. 'Couldn't look after her properly. Left her in an empty house for hours on end. It's no wonder she's disturbed. But you'd think she could show just a little bit of gratitude! It's not many people would have taken her on. Especially at that age.'

'W-what age?' I said.

'Eight years old, she was. It's not easy, adopting a child that age. You'd never believe the trouble they've had with her! Tantrums. Telling lies. You'd have to be a saint to put up with it, if you ask me. What's that?' Nan was peering over my shoulder. 'Knickers!' she said. 'I saw the word knickers! Is that something rude?'

'No!' I hugged the pages to my chest.

'So why are you trying to hide it from me?'

'It's personal,' I said. 'It's s-secret!'

'Hm!' Nan pursed her lips. 'You just watch your step,' she said. 'I'm not saying you shouldn't see her, but . . . just be careful. That's all. You need to take things with a large pinch of salt, where that one's concerned.'

Carefully, I slid Alice's pages back into the Jiffy bag.

'I'm going upstairs, now,' I said. 'I'm not going to hunch! I'm going to r-*read*.'

'That'll make a change,' said Nan.

7

I was rudely woken next morning by the sound of the bedroom door crashing open and heavy footsteps pounding across the floor. I sprang up in bed in a panic. I thought the house must be on fire, or something.

And then I remembered.

'Ch-Charlotte?'

'She's all right!' Nan swept back the curtains. Sunlight came plunging in. 'There's an e-mail from Auntie Marje.' So Nan *could* use the e-mail, when she wanted. She wasn't anywhere near as useless as she made out. 'She's had the op, and she's come through it, and now we just have to wait. But there's every chance it will be a success. So isn't that good?'

'W-w-w—' One of my arms shot out. 'When'll we know?'

'It'll be a while; they can't tell all at once. But we're over the biggest hurdle!' Nan plonked herself down on the bed and enveloped me in a big hug. I did my best not to recoil. 'This is cause for celebration! You and me are going out for the day.'

'What about the shop?' I said.

'Oh, stuff the shop! They can manage without me just

for once. Come on, up you get!'

'What, *now*?' I said. It was only seven o'clock!

'Absolutely! Right away,' said Nan. 'Catch the best of the weather. It's going to rain, later.'

Reluctantly, I swung my legs out of bed. I wasn't sure that I felt ready to celebrate. Not just yet; not until we knew for certain that the operation was going to work. But Nan was obviously set on it.

'Where are we going?' I said.

'Brighton!' said Nan. 'We're going to the seaside. We're going to have fun!'

I guess it was quite fun, in Brighton. It would have been more fun if Alice could have been with us, but after what Nan had said last night I knew better than to suggest it.

'I used to come here with your granddad,' said Nan. 'When we were courting ... used to whizz down on his motor-bike!'

Nan and me had whizzed down by train. Nan was more excited than I'd ever seen her. It was like she'd gone back to when she was young, and courting Granddad. She even wanted to paddle!

'But I won't,' she said, 'if it embarrasses you. I shall go and have an ice cream instead!'

She not only had an ice cream, she had candy floss as well. ('Hm!' she said. 'Doesn't seem to taste the same as it used to.') She also had a great plateful of fish and chips, accompanied by several massive doorsteps of bread and butter and a mug of her horrible brown tea.

She's only quite little. I don't know where she puts it all!

'Oh, this takes me back,' she said. 'Let's go and have a look at the Royal Pavilion! I haven't been there since I was a girl.'

By the time we'd done the Pavilion she reckoned she needed a bit of a sit down and another cup of tea.

'This is the life!' she said. 'Everyone needs a break just now and again. We'll have another, shall we? When your mum gets back with Charlotte.'

Nan seemed in no doubt that Mum *was* going to come back with Charlotte.

'Got to think positively,' she said.

I do try to think positively, but I'm more of a natural worrier than Nan.

'You're like your granddad,' said Nan. 'Never look on the bright side, that was his motto. Every patch of sunshine had a dark cloud behind it.'

In my experience, every patch of sunshine does have a dark cloud behind it, but I didn't say so to Nan. I didn't want to dampen her spirits; it wouldn't be fair.

When we got back home Nan said she was going to go and have a little lie down.

'Not as young as I was . . . unfortunately! What about you? What are you going to do?'

I said that I might go and sit in the garden.

'You mean, go and look for that Alice!' said Nan. 'Go on, then! Off you go. But just remember what I told you.'

I collected Alice's Jiffy bag, not forgetting her *Alice in*

93

Wonderland, which I'd stayed up reading late into the night. I hadn't terribly enjoyed it, to be honest. It's very old-fashioned, and in places I thought it was quite silly. But I'd wanted to prove Nan was wrong. And I had! Alice hadn't copied: she'd *borrowed*. That's quite a different thing. What she'd done, she'd taken some of the characters and she'd used them to tell her story. *Her* story. I was eager to let her know that I'd read it.

I hoisted myself up on to the wall. My eyes swivelled automatically in the direction of the fox earth, but I could see no sign of her. At least she hadn't disappeared again down her rabbit hole.

'Alice!' I called. 'Are you there?'

'Oddball!' She came bounding up the garden and hurled herself at the wall. 'Where have you been? I've been looking for you!'

I explained about Brighton, and about Charlotte's operation. How Nan had wanted to go and celebrate.

'Didn't you want to, as well?' said Alice.

'N-never look on the b-bright side,' I said. 'That was my granddad's motto. I think I m-must take after him.'

'I look on the bright side,' said Alice. 'Whenever I can. I like to pretend good things might happen. They don't, very often. But just sometimes they do. And then it's a nice surprise! Have you read my story? What did you think of it?'

I said I thought that it was really good. 'Really w-well written and imaginat-t-t–'

'–tive,' said Alice.

'And c-clever,' I said. ' 'Cos I read one of the b-books, as well.'

'Did you like it?'

I said yes; quite. 'But not as m-much as yours! Yours made me l-laugh.'

Alice said, 'Laugh?' Her voice had gone all tight. Too late, I knew that I had said the wrong thing.

'Y-yeah. W-well . . .' I faltered. 'In p-parts,' I said.

'Which parts?'

'The . . . um . . . knickers?' I said. 'Off with her knickers!'

Alice narrowed her eyes. 'You thought that was funny?'

'W-well . . . s-sort of,' I said.

'Yes.' Alice nodded. 'I can see it might seem funny to someone with a warped sense of humour.'

'I didn't mean f-funny ha-ha,' I said, quickly. 'I meant f-funny like . . . qu-quirky. Qu-*quirky* funny.'

Alice was looking at me.

'Unusual,' I said. '*Interesting*. But of course,' I added, humbly, 'I c-couldn't p-properly underst-tand it all.'

'Why not?' said Alice. 'I suppose you mean you didn't *want* to!'

'I did!' I said. 'It's j-just . . .'

'Just what?'

'I wasn't qu-quite sure . . .' My voice trailed off. A sense of sudden misery engulfed me. I'd upset her! I'd failed her. She'd entrusted me with her precious story, and I'd let her down.

'Oh, never mind! It doesn't matter.' Alice grabbed her

95

Jiffy bag and sprang, impatiently, off the wall. 'Boobs! Bottom! Bum! D'you want to come and have tea with us?'

My heart did this lurching thing that I thought only happened in books. She wasn't mad at me! She'd forgiven me.

'D'you want to?' she said.

I nodded, gratefully. I wasn't actually very hungry after all the fish and chips and ice cream, but I didn't feel like going back indoors. I didn't even feel like hunching over the computer.

'L-look!' I said. 'I got you a p-present.'

'Ooh, a stick of rock! Thank you,' said Alice. 'That'll come in handy for bashing Sarah.'

'I got it for you to *eat*,' I said.

'I'll bash first and eat later,' she said.

Alice's mum and dad were both back from work. They were in the kitchen, already seated at the table, along with Sarah and Granny Gregory. Alice announced in ringing tones that she had invited me to tea.

'If that's all right?'

Her mum said that I could come to tea as often as I liked but had I asked my nan? I explained that Nan was upstairs in her room, having a lie down after Brighton.

'I still think you ought to ask her,' insisted Alice's mum. 'She's going to be worried if she wakes up and you're not there.'

'Oh, let the boy eat!' Alice's dad pulled out a chair and slapped a hand on the seat. 'Sit yourself down, young man! I'll make it all right with your nan. I'll pop round and see her on my way out. Now, here's a joke! *Waiter, waiter! There's a worm in my pie.* Then you say—' he pointed his fork at me '— *It's fat, sir.*'

'It's f-f-fat, sir.'

'*I'm not surprised! It's eaten all the pastry!*'

Alice groaned and said, '*Dad!* That's *awful!*' Sarah screamed, and banged her spoon on the table. Alice's mum gave a faint smile, but was obviously still fussing about Nan.

'So long as she doesn't wake up and wonder where he is before you get round there,' she said.

Alice pulled a face. Alice's dad rolled his eyes.

'Here's another one! Here's another one!' He leaned across the table. 'What did one magnet say to another?'

'Um . . . I d-don't know,' I said.

'*Wrong!*' Alice's dad turned to Alice and Sarah. 'Come on, you girls! Tell him the answer . . . what did one magnet say to another?'

'*I find you very attractive.*' They chanted it, in unison.

'What did the high tide say to the low tide?'

'*Lo, tide!*'

'What did the low tide say to the high tide?'

'*Hi, tide!*'

'And what happened next?'

'Nothing! They just waved at each other!'

I laughed. Not at the jokes themselves – I mean, they were the sort of thing you read in comics when you're about six – but at Alice's dad. He had this roguish grin on his face, and his beard kept waggling. I can't ever remember my dad telling jokes. I guess he might have done, in the old days, before I arrived on the scene and started stammering and stuttering and causing him grief. He was probably quite different in those days. Well, he must have been, or Mum wouldn't have married him. It was me that went and ruined everything.

After tea, Alice's dad announced that he was going to organize the clearing away and the washing-up.

'Whose turn is it to wash? Alice, I believe it's yours. Sarah, it's your turn to wipe. Your mother can sit down and have a well-earned rest. Young man!' He pinched my ear, jovially, between finger and thumb. 'You can help me put things away.'

'He'll only drop them,' said Sarah.

'He'll do no such thing,' said her dad. 'You won't drop them, will you, young man?'

'He will!' shrieked Sarah. 'He's got a twitch!'

And then she let out a scream as Alice pinched her, viciously, on the arm.

'Daaaaad! She's pinching me!'

I could feel that my face had gone very red. Alice's dad said, 'Alice!' Alice subsided, immediately. 'Sarah!' Sarah chewed at a fingernail. 'Let us get on with the task in hand. Young master! Your job is to take the things from Sarah as she wipes them and to lay them down, *so.*' He picked up a fork and placed it on the table. 'I will put them away where they belong. This is what is known as team work. Are you ready? Then let the water pour!'

I reckoned Nan would be impressed when I told her how Big Norm helped with the washing-up. Her constant cry when Granddad had been alive was, 'That man never lifts a finger!' My dad never lifted much of a finger, either. But Alice's dad supervised the whole operation. He scrutinized every item, checking for signs of sloppy washing-up. He told Alice that she was using too much washing-up liquid and not enough elbow grease, and Sarah that she wasn't wiping properly.

'If a job is worth doing, it is worth doing well. No task is too humble. What does the Queen do when she burps, young man?'

I almost dropped a plate that Sarah was handing me. I caught it just in time. 'I d-d-d-d—'

'You don't know? Tell him, girls!'

'She issues a royal pardon!'

Even washing-up was fun with Big Norm. It was silly – but it was fun. I felt quite sorry when it was finished and he had to go out.

'I'll drop by your nan and tell her where you are. You stay here and the girls will entertain you.'

'He's got to go and visit someone from the church,' said Alice. 'He's got to go and sit with them. D'you want to come up to my room?'

'You're not allowed!' shrilled Sarah. 'He said we *both* had to entertain!'

'Well, go on, then,' said Alice. 'Entertain!'

Sarah put her finger in her mouth.

'Has your dad gone?' Alice's mum had appeared at

the kitchen door. 'Come into the other room, Duffy. Come on, you two! We have a guest. What shall we do to amuse him?'

Alice said, 'Let's play the acting game!'

'All right,' said her mum. 'If that's what you want. But just remember it's not a competition.' She sent a warning glance at Alice. 'Just a game.'

I didn't want to play any games! Especially not an acting game. How could I play an acting game? When I couldn't even say two words without tripping over my own tongue? I stared reproachfully at Alice. I felt betrayed! How could she do this to me?

She obviously guessed what I was thinking because she giggled and said, 'Don't look so worried, Oddball! You don't have to *say* things. It's all in dumb show. See, what we do, we choose the title of a book, or a TV show, or something, and we break it into syllables and we act it out, and everyone has to guess what it is. It's easy!'

I still felt appalled. I reckon I make quite enough of a spectacle of myself as it is, without adding to it. But it seemed this was the sort of family that invented its own games. If you wanted to be one of them, you had to join in.

I was quite surprised at Alice's mum, to be honest I'd never have thought she'd be the kind to get up and do things in front of people. But she acted *Buffy the Vampire Slayer* without even batting an eyelid. It didn't seem to bother her, making a fool of herself. Alice cried, '*Mum-u-um!* That's terrible!' Sarah screeched, and buried her face in a cushion.

'Mum can't act to save her life,' said Alice.

Her mum wasn't the only one. I can't, either! But after that, I couldn't really get out of it. Feeling horribly self-conscious, I mimed *The Lord of the Rings*, which made Sarah shriek again and clutch at her cushion.

'See?' said Alice. 'I told you . . . nothing to be scared of!'

Second time around, I did *The Hobbit*. I was feeling a bit more confident by now and almost starting to enjoy it. Alice's mum was about to embark on her third one – 'Book title' – when the door was thrown open and Big Norm appeared.

'Dad!' Both girls hurled themselves at him. It was like he'd been away for an entire month, instead of just over an hour. I couldn't help wondering how it would feel, to have a dad you were that close to. A dad you could run and greet, and throw your arms around. I had this feeling that Nan was right: Alice *ought* to be a bit more grateful.

'What are you playing? The acting game? Splendid!' Alice's dad rubbed his hands together. 'Shall I take over? What do we have? Whisper in my ear!' Alice's mum obediently did so. 'Aha! A book title. Seven words. Right! First word—' He made one of his hands into a fist. I'd learnt that that meant the first word was *the*. 'Second word—' Alice's dad dropped to all fours and began to prowl the room, waving his head from side to side and gnashing with his teeth. Sarah shrieked louder than ever and stuffed her hand into her mouth.

'Lion!' cried Alice. And in my ear she confided, 'Dad's

brilliant!' And then, 'I can guess what it is but I want to see him do it!'

The third word was *the* again. For the fourth word, Alice's dad mimed a tall pointy hat, swished at an invisible cloak, mounted an invisible broomstick, crossed his eyes and twisted his lips into a leer.

'I know what it is, I know what it is!' Sarah was jumping up and down. 'It's *The Lion, the Witch and the Wardrobe*!'

Her mum, ruefully, said, 'Your dad's too good, I'm afraid. He puts the rest of us in the shade.'

'Told you he was brilliant,' hissed Alice.

'Do some more! Do some more!' Sarah threw herself on to the sofa and kicked up her legs. 'Do another funny one!'

'I think I'll make a cup of tea,' said Alice's mum. 'What time does Duffy have to be back?'

'Oh, any time! Don't worry about it, I'll walk him round,' said Big Norm. 'Now, let's see . . . let me try and think of another one. All right, here we go! Song title. Five words. First word—'

It was past ten o'clock when Alice's dad walked back round the block with me. Nan was already in her dressing gown and nightdress, ready for bed.

'My dear Mrs Chambers!' Alice's dad was full of apologies. 'I hope we haven't kept you up?'

'No, no!' said Nan. 'I'm still glued to the box. I just hope Duffy didn't outstay his welcome?'

'Not at all! We could have kept going all night, couldn't we?'

I reckoned we could. It was what you might call a novel experience for me, all the family playing games.

After Alice's dad had gone, I said to Nan, 'He's b-brilliant! He could be on telly!'

'Oh, he's got the gift,' said Nan. 'No doubt about that!'

8

'Hi Oddball!'

Alice was on her usual perch, at the end of the garden.

'Yo!' I raised a hand in salute. She waved back at me. 'How ya doing?' I said.

I was feeling good. I was feeling *positive*. It was the first morning I'd woken up in a long time without a great black cloud hanging over me. I guessed it was something to do with last night. Laughing at all the jokes. Playing the mime game. Being part of a family. I wasn't even worried about Charlotte any more. Well, I was, deep down; but at least I'd been able to bury it a bit. She'd had the operation, and that was the biggest hurdle.

I swung myself up on to the wall.

'Horse dung!' said Alice.

'Bumhole,' I said.

'Putrefaction!'

'*Excrement.*'

'Muck and mess and piles of sick!' Alice collapsed into giggles. 'This is so disgusting!'

We were being pretty childish. But so what?

'S-s-s-*quitters!*' She beamed at me. 'I like having Tourette's!'

'You wouldn't,' I said, 'if you r-really had it.'

'Well, maybe not,' said Alice. 'But it's fun to pretend! Like last night ... that was fun, wasn't it? Everyone pretending.'

'Your dad's really funny,' I said.

'Our dad makes everyone laugh.'

'My nan,' I said, 'has got this thing about him.'

'They all have,' said Alice. 'All the old ladies. In the church. They all have things. They think he's the dog's bollocks.'

I choked. I should have been used to Alice by now, but she still sometimes took me by surprise. There she sat, all sweet and demure, with her little round face and her big cornflower eyes, looking like an angel off the top of the Christmas tree – and then she opened her mouth and poured out sewage. Sewage is what Nan calls it.

'Don't you come that sewage with me young man!' It's what she always says if she catches me swearing. And that's only *ordinary* swearwords such as damn and blast.

Alice shrieked, 'Look at you!'

Hastily, I rearranged my features. I didn't want her thinking she'd shocked me. She hadn't shocked me. I was unshockable!

Changing the subject, I said, 'Hey! Guess what? I've written a poem!'

'*You* have?' said Alice.

'Y-yeah.' I nodded, suddenly bashful. 'D'you want to see it?'

'Yes!'

I stuffed my hand into the back pocket of my jeans and pulled out the scrappy bit of paper which was all I'd been able to find when the poem had burst upon me. As I explained to Alice, I'd woken up at six o'clock – practically unheard of! – with the poem whizzing about my head. I don't normally go for poems. Poems are not my scene.

'But it just, like . . . c-came to me. Out of n-nowhere.'

'The best poems often do,' said Alice.

'I've never written one bef-f-f—'

'-fore,' said Alice. 'And what do *you* want?' she demanded, as Sarah came lumbering up the garden.

'Don't want anything,' said Sarah.

'So just go away,' said Alice. She flapped a hand. 'We're busy!'

'Why?' said Sarah. 'What are you doing?'

'None of your business! It's private.'

'Private's the same as secret, and you're not allowed to have secrets!' shrilled Sarah.

Alice tossed her head. 'I can be secret if I want! Just naff off and leave us alone.'

'Won't!' Sarah took up a defiant stance, just in front of the wall, staring her challenge at Alice.

'If you don't shove off,' said Alice, 'I'll get down and bash you.'

'Better hadn't,' said Sarah. 'You touch me and you'll be in trouble, you will!'

Alice's ivory cheeks turned slowly scarlet. 'I'm warning you,' she said.

106

'Yes, and Dad warned you! You're just jealous,' shrieked Sarah, ' 'cos he likes me best! 'Cos I'm good and you're not! You're evil, you are!'

With a bloodcurdling screech, Alice jumped down off the wall and launched herself at Sarah. I watched, in a kind of horrified fascination, as the two of them rolled together on the ground, kicking, biting, clawing. Sarah's shrieks filled the air. Alice fought in grim silence. She seemed intent on pulling out her sister's hair by the roots. I couldn't help remembering what Steven had said . . . *That Alice, she's a total nutter.*

I was just reaching out nervously, to try to separate them when Granny Gregory appeared with a length of garden cane in her hand.

'Alice! You stop that!' She raised the cane and brought it down with a sharp *whack* across the back of Alice's bare legs. 'Sarah come here!'

Sarah flew to her, sobbing.

'Get back indoors,' said Granny Gregory. 'And you, miss!' She shook the cane at Alice. 'You just wait till your father hears!'

Still sniffling, Sarah trailed back up the garden. I felt a bit shaken, to tell the truth; I'd never seen girls fight like that before. Alice on the other hand seemed quite unperturbed. She scrambled back on to the wall and made a rude gesture in the direction of Sarah's departing back.

'Dickhead! Well, come on, then!' She held out a hand. 'Where's your poem?'

Reluctantly, I let her have it. I was beginning to wish I'd never mentioned it; not with Alice in this mood. To my shame, just to make matters worse, she insisted on reading it out loud. I bleated a protest, but she didn't take any notice.

'I always read things out loud,' she said.

She wasn't the sort of girl you could argue with. I wasn't scared she'd hit me, or anything. I'm not that much of a coward! It was just . . . for such a tiny creature, she couldn't half be overbearing.

'Poem for Charlotte,' announced Alice.

I cringed. And went on cringing.

> *'Baby sister Charlotte,*
> *With your soft brown hair,*
> *What have you done to deserve to be ill?*
> *Life is so unfair!*
>
> *I think of you last thing at night,*
> *And when I wake at dawn.*
> *I have loved you, oh so much!*
> *Since the day that you were born.*
>
> *Please get better very soon*
> *And come back home to me.*
> *Come back from California,*
> *Across the wide blue sea.'*

By the time she'd finished I was just about ready to dig

a hole and bury myself. My whole body was squirming with embarrassment. I'd been so proud of that poem at six o'clock in the morning! Now it just seemed . . . yucky. I didn't dare ask Alice what she thought, her being the expert and all; but being Alice she told me, anyway.

'Well, it's not a specially *good* poem,' she said, 'but it's got lots of good feelings, and that's what counts . . . good feelings. You obviously love her very much.'

I swallowed. 'Y-yes,' I said. 'I do!'

'See, that's what matters,' said Alice. 'Loving her. And being able to tell her so.'

'Even b-badly?' I said.

'Even badly,' said Alice. 'Though it's not as bad as all that,' she added, kindly. 'It scans quite nicely. But even if it didn't, that's not the point. The point is, you've written it down. And it helps,' said Alice, 'to write things down. Leastways, *I* think it does.'

I nodded, humbly. I was prepared to accept Alice's word when it came to poetry. I stuffed the paper into my pocket and hoisted myself back on the wall.

'I think you ought to keep it,' said Alice, 'for when she's older. Then you can show it to her.'

I frowned, and my arm shot out. 'She m-might th-think it was s-s-*soppy*.'

'She wouldn't.' Alice said it very firmly. 'She'd think it was beautiful. Anyone would think it was beautiful! It's a love poem. I can't write love poems, I'm not nice enough. When you're a horrid sort of person, you can only write horrid sort of things. I've done another chapter of my book, by the way. Wait there, I'll get it.'

Alice slid off the wall and disappeared, on all fours, into the undergrowth. Within seconds, she was back.

'I brought it with me,' she said. 'I put it down the hole. It's where I keep it now.' Carefully, she unrolled some sheets of paper wrapped in a scroll, in a plastic food bag. 'I didn't want it to get dirty. Or for *her* to find it. Shall I read it to you?'

I said all right, since she obviously wanted to, but I have to be honest: I'd have rather she didn't. I felt like it was some kind of a test, and I was really scared in case I might fail.

'Don't looked so worried,' said Alice. 'It's only a *story*.'

'You mean, a m-made up s-story?' I said.

There was a pause.

'A *story*,' said Alice. She cleared her throat.

'Chapter Five

    "You! Girl!" called a voice.

    It seemed to be coming from somewhere in a tree. Alice looked up. She saw a Cheshire Cat stretched out along one of the branches.

    "You!" said the Cat. It waved a paw in Alice's direction.

    "Me?" said Alice.

    "Yes, you!" said the Cat. "Who else is there?"

    Alice had to admit, there wasn't anyone.

    "Well, there you are, then," said the Cat. It stifled a yawn with one paw. "I'm bored!" it said.

    "I'm sorry to hear that," said Alice, determined to be polite.

"So you ought to be," said the Cat. "Wandering about with your head in the clouds."

"Pardon me, but my head is nowhere near the clouds," objected Alice. "In fact—" she put up her hand to shade her eyes "— there is not a cloud anywhere to be seen."

"That is totally beside the point," said the Cat. It was beginning to sound a trifle irritable. "Wake your ideas up! Shift yourself! Do something to amuse me."

"Such as what?" said Alice.

"That depends what you are capable of."

"Nothing very much, I'm afraid," said Alice, sadly. "At least, that is what everyone tells me, so I suppose it must be true."

"You mean, you can't do ANYTHING?" The Cat tutted, crossly. "You must have some social accomplishments!"

"I could recite a poem," said Alice. "Would that amuse you?"

"It might," said the Cat, rather grudgingly. "You could always try."

"Very well," said Alice.

The Cat settled itself into a listening position, with its front paws tucked beneath its chest.

"Poem," said Alice.

" 'Twas even and the slippy slovs
Did sloop and slither in the slobe.
All twinky were the rosytovs,
And the mumsy mims misgove.

"Beware the jab-jab thing, my son!
The sword that stabs, the fangs that bite.

111

The greedy grabbing hands that come
In the darkness of the night.

"Beware the slippy slobbering,
The gobble and the guzzle.
Chastise your child when she is wild
And put her in a muzzle."

"There!" said Alice. "What did you think of that?"

"Rather dark," said the Cat. "And why was the first verse written in a foreign tongue?"

"It is what is known as a nonsense rhyme," explained Alice. "You make up words for the sound of them."

"And what, may one ask, is the point of that?"

Alice wasn't quite sure, to tell the truth.

"I think it is just for fun," she said. "Perhaps I should try another one?"

"If you must," said the Cat. "So long as it is composed in the English language."

Alice thought hard. "I know!" she cried. "I've got one!"

But the Cat had disappeared. Alice could have wept with vexation.

"Why do I bother?" she thought. "What is the point of trying? Nobody cares. It really is too bad!"

'Well,' said Alice. The real Alice. She rolled the pages back into a scroll. 'What do you think?'

I still had this feeling that I was on trial.

'It's a s-story,' I said. 'R-right?'

'I told you,' said Alice.

'But a m-made up one?'

'I didn't copy it,' said Alice, 'if that's what you're thinking! People are always accusing me of copying things, but I don't. I make them up. In here.' She tapped her head.

'So it's all just inv-vented?' I said.

'It's all in my own words. *They* don't think I've got the brain. But I have! I could have gone to the High School if they'd only let me sit the entrance exam. I'd have passed, easy as pie! I could have got a scholarship. But they wouldn't let me, 'cos of *her*.'

'You mean, S-Sarah?' I said.

'S-S-*Sarah*. Just 'cos she's got no brain, I'm not supposed to have one, either. 'Cos it wouldn't be fair if I had one and she didn't! I'm not allowed to do anything she can't. So now we both have to go to this dump place. What did you think of the poem? *Beware the slippy slobbering, The gobble and the guzzle . . .*'

'Is it meant to be a n-nightmare?' I said.

Alice put her head on one side. She looked at me. 'Does it sound like a nightmare?'

I said, 'Yeah!' and braced myself for attack. I'd probably gone and got it wrong again. But for once, it seemed, I'd said the right thing.

'That's exactly what it is,' said Alice. 'It's a nightmare!' She leapt down off the wall. '*They're* going out shopping. They'll have gone by now. D'you want to do something for me? D'you want to come and help me put a lock on my bedroom door?'

'A l-lock?' I said. 'On your b-bedroom?'

'To stop the nightmares,' said Alice. 'So that I can be private. That's all I want . . . I just want to be *private*. I've already got all the stuff. I've got a bolt. Look!'

She dug a hand into the pocket of her shorts and produced a small brass bolt.

'There's a hammer and a screwdriver and stuff in the kitchen . . . I just need someone to help me. Will you? *Please*? Oddball? Will you?'

I supposed it was all right, helping Alice put a bolt on her bedroom door. After all, it was her bedroom. And it was only quite a small bolt.

'*Please*?' said Alice.

'Well, if you r-reckon it's OK,' I said.

'It doesn't matter whether it's OK! It's got to be done. 'Cos if it's *not* . . .' said Alice.

'W-what?'

'Something terrible might happen!'

I guess I had these visions of Alice with her hands round Sarah's throat. Tearing her hair out. Gouging her eyes out. I guess I thought that was what she meant.

'OK,' I said. 'L-let's go and do it.'

It didn't take long, just to fix one small bolt. I am not the world's greatest when it comes to DIY, but I reckoned I'd made a pretty neat job of it.

'Oh, that is brilliant!' cried Alice. She flew at me, and planted a big smacker of a kiss on my cheek. 'Thank you, thank you, thank you! Dear darling Oddball! I knew you'd help me!'

I tried to say, 'Don't mention it,' in a lordly, offhand kind of way, but could get no further than 'D-d-d-d' and had to give up. I went back to Nan's for lunch with my cheek pulsating where she'd kissed me. It was, actually, to be honest, the first time I'd ever been kissed by a girl. I guess I was glad that it was Alice.

I spent the afternoon hunched over the computer and was still there at five o'clock when Nan came running up the stairs and burst into the room going, 'What on earth is happening out there?'

I hadn't been aware that anything was happening. Sometimes when I'm on the computer I get a bit lost, out there in cyberspace, and tend to forget the everyday world. It wasn't till Nan threw open the window and leaned out that I heard it: the sound of voices, raised in anger. I joined Nan at the window.

'It's that Alice,' said Nan.

From the window of the spare room we could see down the garden, and into Alice's garden at the end. I could just make out the figures of Alice and her mum. It looked as if Alice had run into the garden and her mum had run after her. Her mum had hold of her and was shouting: 'We don't do that sort of thing in this house!'

I heard Alice shouting back: 'I just want to be private! Why can't I be private?'

'Who is it you want to be private from?' Now her mum had her by the shoulders and was shaking her to and fro. '*Who is it?*'

'S-Sarah,' I said. 'It's S-Sarah!'

115

Nan closed the window. 'That child,' she said.

'It's n-not her fault!' I felt the need to stick up for Alice. Sometimes it seemed like everybody had it in for her. I told Nan how she'd begged me to help her put a bolt on her bedroom door. 'It's because of Sarah! She keeps bursting in.'

'All the same,' said Nan.

'But it's not f-fair!'

'What isn't?' said Nan.

I said, 'The way they're always having a g-go at Alice and making excuses for S-Sarah!'

'Well, of course they do,' said Nan. 'That poor little soul's got enough to cope with. Alice at least has all her wits about her. She ought to see for herself that Sarah's no competition.'

'She told Alice that their dad didn't love Alice as much as he loves her.'

'Well, now, that's just not true! And no one in their right mind could ever think that it was. He's treated those girls exactly alike. He's always said, right from the word go, he would never do for one what he wouldn't do for the other.'

'Like Alice not being allowed to try for the High School,' I said.

'Try for the High School?' Nan laughed. 'This is fantasy time, this is! She'd never get in there. Not in a million years!'

'She m-might have done.' I thought of Alice's story. The words she used. The poems she wrote. *I didn't copy*

116

it, if that's what you're thinking! 'If they'd just let her t-try,' I said.

'What yarns has she been spinning you?' said Nan. 'I warned you, didn't I? That girl is not to be trusted. You have to take everything she says with a large pinch of salt.'

'But she's c-clever!' I said.

'Oh, yes! She's clever, all right . . . clever at getting her own way. Getting people like you to help her do things she has no right to be doing. Putting a bolt on her bedroom door! What do you think your mum would say if she found you screwing things into the woodwork? I'm surprised at you! But I suppose she sweet-talked you,' said Nan. 'She can put it on, when she wants. Looks,' said Nan, 'can be very deceiving. It's a case of butter wouldn't melt in the mouth when she wants something of you. Other times – well! You've seen for yourself. You don't need me to tell you.'

Later in the evening, I wandered down the garden and peered over the wall.

'Alice?' I whispered; but she wasn't there. I could see Sarah, playing with the kittens on the lawn. I nearly called out to her, but then at the last minute decided against it. I'd only start yammering and stammering. I didn't mind doing it in front of Alice; but not Sarah.

I turned, and went back indoors. Alice would be there in the morning.

9

She wasn't! I looked for her, but she was nowhere about. I looked again in the middle of the morning, and again just before Nan got back from work, and again before tea and again after. I didn't feel quite bold enough to go climbing over the wall to check whether she was down the rabbit hole. I didn't *think* she was. I peered as hard as I could, but could see no sign.

It wasn't a bad sort of day. It started off with an e-mail from Mum saying how Charlotte was doing really well; how she and Auntie Marje and the doctors were all keeping their fingers crossed. She said things were 'looking good', so that cheered me up. I just wished I could go and share it with Alice!

I spent the morning hunched over the machine (when I wasn't down the garden, peering over the wall) and the afternoon at the cinema with Nan. It was Nan's idea.

'I haven't been to the cinema since I can't remember when,' she said. 'I never could get your granddad to go. Let's see what's on!'

We had a look in the local paper and quite honestly there wasn't anything suitable for a person of Nan's age.

Not what I would consider suitable. I felt she'd like something soft and romantic, and all there was was *The Mummy Returns* and a rerun of *Star Wars: The Empire Strikes Back*.

'That'll do,' said Nan. 'That *Star Wars* thing. I suppose you've already seen it? Well, never mind! It won't hurt you to see it again. I'm certainly not going to some horror film about a mummy, thank you very much!'

'It's not a horror film,' I said. 'It's supposed to be funny.' But Nan still insisted on *Star Wars*. She slays me at times! She really does. She said she wanted to know what all the fuss was about.

'That Obi Wanker Nobby, whatever his name is.'

'Obi-Wan K-Kenobi,' I said.

'Whatever,' said Nan.

She doesn't just slay me, she *double* slays me. I stored it up to tell Alice. Alice would appreciate it! We laughed at the same things, her and me. A day without seeing her was like a day without a Kit Kat. I am addicted to Kit Kats. I am a Kit Kat junkie! Mum has to limit me to two fingers a day, otherwise I would just gorge. Maybe I was becoming addicted to Alice, too? I needed her to keep my spirits up. I needed her giggles and her sparkiness. The way she had opinions about everything under the sun. The way she called me Oddball. The way she finished my sentences for me. The swearing game. Even her bursts of rage. (They were all part of her, and they all kept me on my toes.)

Come Friday I looked for her again, but she still wasn't

there. I was beginning to get a bit worried. What could have happened to her? After some dithering I turned to G in Nan's telephone book and found the telephone number, and after some more dithering I picked up the receiver and dialled it. But nobody answered and by then it was one o'clock and Nan had come back from work and I didn't like to try while she was there. I don't know why; I guess I just felt it was something private between me and Alice.

On Saturday Nan said that in the afternoon she had a fancy to take a drive in the car.

'I thought we might go over to Box Hill. It's one of the first places I ever went to with your granddad. I'd like to see Box Hill again.'

I couldn't work out whether she was making all this effort because she felt she had to entertain me, or whether it was something she really wanted to do.

'Is that all right?' she said. 'Box Hill this afternoon . . . what about this morning? What are you going to do this morning?'

I said I hadn't decided yet. 'I might go and s-see Alice.'

I waited for Nan to say, 'Why not invite her to come along with us?', but of course she didn't. She just tightened her lips like she always did.

'Don't you go climbing over that wall,' she said. 'You go round the front and knock on the door – and make sure you're back in time for lunch!'

I had a quick check over the wall, just in case, but Alice still wasn't around.

'I told you,' said Nan, 'go round the front . . . What is it with you people and doors? Have you forgotten what they're for? Anyone would think you'd been brought up in a tent!'

It was Alice's dad who opened the door to me. He was wearing a little frilly apron tied round his waist and a red T-shirt with the words WHY NOT COME ROUND MY PLACE SUNDAY? GOD. I couldn't make up my mind whether it was really neat or really yucky, but either way I was impressed. I would die sooner than make a spectacle of myself! I reckoned Alice's dad had to be a pretty strong person with pretty strong beliefs. I admired him for that.

'Aha!' he cried, when he saw it was me. ' 'Tis the young master! Come in, young man, come in! You're just in time.'

I wanted to say, 'I've come to see Alice,' but I found myself being bundled down the hall and into the kitchen before I could get the words out. Granny Gregory was in the kitchen, polishing silver. Sarah was standing at the stove, stirring something in a big pan.

'Right! Give me the spoon.' Her dad took it from her and pushed her in the direction of the door. 'Go and fetch the others. Tell them we're ready. Sarah and I,' he informed me, 'have been making toffee. We are about to have a tasting. Fill that bowl with cold water.'

He gestured to a bowl on the kitchen table. Obediently I carried it over to the sink.

'What we do, we take a spoonful of goo, like so . . . and we drop it! Into the water. Splish, splosh! There it

121

goes. See? How it firms up? Now we'll drop some more.'

I watched in fascination as dobs of molten toffee fell with a series of plops into the bowl. Imagine having a dad who made toffee! A dad who wasn't ashamed to wear a frilly apron . . .

Sarah came back with her mum and two other people with a couple of small children. But not Alice. Where *was* Alice? I didn't like to ask, in front of so many people. Especially strangers. I'd only make a fool of myself.

Alice's mum said, 'Duffy! How are you this morning?'

I mumbled that I was fine, thank you.

'Let me introduce you . . . These are Mr and Mrs Nunnelly, from our congregation. These are Jo and Susie. Everyone, this is Duffy, Mrs Chambers' grandson.'

The two grown-ups both shook hands and said how nice it was to meet me.

'We've heard so much about you!'

The kids just stared, so I didn't bother saying anything to them; it seemed safer that way. I still wondered where Alice was.

'Outside! Everyone outside! Time to begin. Ceremonial tasting!'

Holding aloft his bowl of toffee, Alice's dad led the way into the garden. We all meekly followed. He was one of those people who just naturally took charge. He set the bowl on top of the bird table and told Sarah to 'Run and get some saucepan lids! As many as you can. We need some music.'

Sarah ran back indoors and excitedly ran back out

again with a collection of lids, which her dad promptly began handing round.

'Come along, you young people! Let's have a bit of noise. Sarah, take the spoon . . . You're on the triangle. Young man!' He snatched up a plastic bucket and thrust it at me. 'You're on the drums. You two, you little ones! Clash those saucepan lids. Clash them with all your might! Are we ready? Ta-ra, ta-ra! Wagons . . . roll!'

We all set off round the bird table, Alice's dad in the lead, making loud trumpeting noises into his clenched fist, Sarah battering at her saucepan lid with the spoon, Jo and Susie clashing their cymbals and me in the rear, half-heartedly thumping on my plastic bucket. I felt very self-conscious. I felt like a total idiot. I wouldn't have minded so much if Alice had been there. Without her it just seemed . . . *childish*.

'Ta-ra ta-ra! Where's that drum? I don't hear any drum! Keep those cymbals going!'

He paraded us twice round the bird table, then down to the end of the garden. (I threw a quick glance towards the rabbit hole, but Alice didn't seem to be there.) When we arrived back at the terrace, the assembled grown-ups all broke into loud applause. *Way* over the top. I reckoned they were just currying favour with Big Norm.

'Oh, dear!' The Mrs Nunnelly person came over to talk to me as we all stood around chomping toffee. She laughed. 'This is real stick-jaw stuff, isn't it?'

I nodded, glad of the excuse not to have to say anything.

123

'But quite delicious! Norman is a champion sweet-maker. And he is so funny! Don't you think?'

I nodded again.

'The things he gets up to! Oh, my! Look at him now.'

Alice's dad had two saucepan lids clamped to his chest and was doing a hula-hula dance round the bird table, waggling his hips.

'He has us all in stitches! It must be such a comfort to your gran, him living so close. And it must be nice for you, too! Like a second family.'

I sucked toffee off the roof of my mouth and stashed it to one side. I said, 'I'm Alice's f-f-friend, really.'

'Yes.' Her smile faded. 'Alice . . . it's such a shame about Alice! They've tried so hard with her. Even Norman can't seem to get through.'

I could. I could get through to her!

'He'll never give up, you know. No, thank you, dear.' She shook her head as Sarah pushed another lump of toffee at her. 'He'll persist, no matter what it takes. The harder she tries to push him away, the harder he'll work at it. He sees it as a challenge. He won't be beaten. How is your little sister, by the way? How is she doing? We've all been praying for her. We've been so worried! Have you heard from your mum?'

Before I could manage to form any words in reply, Alice's dad was calling out in his usual hearty tones that it was 'Time for the off!'. Mrs Nunnelly said, 'Oh! I'm afraid we have to leave. Norman's very kindly giving us a lift into town. We mustn't keep him waiting.' I was glad about that; I didn't feel like talking to anyone about Charlotte. Alice was the only person I could talk to. Well, apart from Nan. Even then, I felt more comfortable with Alice.

When they'd all gone, and I was on my own with just Sarah and her mum, I finally plucked up courage to ask the question I'd been wanting to ask all along: 'Is A-Alice ar-round?'

'No, she's not!' shrilled Sarah. 'She's—'

'Sarah, take all these things back indoors,' said her mum. 'Then go upstairs and tell Alice she can come down . . . tell her Duffy's here.'

Sarah, practically bursting at the seams with self-righteousness, went scuttling back into the house. Her mum said, 'I'm afraid Alice is in disgrace.' She said it almost like she was apologizing for it. 'Her dad didn't want her at the ceremony.'

'Is it b-b-b—' I clenched my fists. 'Is it because of the p-padlock? Bec-cause if it *is*—'

'She had no right to do it!' said her mum.

'B-but it was p-partly my fault!' I said. 'I h-helped her!'

'You weren't to know. Nobody's blaming you. But Alice should certainly have known better than to do such a thing. We're not that sort of family! We don't have secrets from one another. We're *a family*. You surely don't have a padlock on your bedroom door, do you?'

I had to admit that I didn't; but it was different for me! I didn't have a sister like Sarah, who kept invading my privacy. I tried to explain.

'Sh-sh-she—'

If I could only just open my mouth and speak, the same as anyone else! It seemed to me that someone had to defend Alice. And I was her friend, so it was up to me.

I got as far as the first few explosions – 'She w-w-was only t-t-t-t—' – when Alice herself appeared sullenly at the back door.

'It's all right,' said her mum. 'You can come out. Your father's gone into town with the Nunnellys. He won't be back till later. But he's still very upset by your behaviour!'

Alice didn't say a word. She just walked straight past us, and on down the garden. Her mum sighed.

'It would be an enormous help,' she said, 'if you could get her to apologize.'

'M-me?' I said.

'She might listen to you; she takes no notice of anything *I* say. What she did was extremely hurtful! Her dad's not angry with her, he just feels wounded. He's waiting for her to go to him. To tell him that she's sorry. That's all!'

I wasn't sure that I could ask that of Alice. I wasn't really sure what she had done that was so terrible. I could see that fixing a padlock to your bedroom door and ruining the paintwork might not exactly be guaranteed to send your parents into ecstasies; but it didn't strike me as being a capital offence. I couldn't see what was *hurtful* about it. Alice just wanted some privacy!

I found her, as I knew I would, down the hole. Sitting

there with her knees hunched up to her chin. I crawled in beside her.

'Hi!'

Alice remained silent.

I said, 'I l-looked for you yesterday. But you w-weren't here!'

Still she stayed silent.

'I w-wanted to t-talk to you!'

Slowly, she turned her head to look at me. 'Why?'

' 'Cos I like talking to you! It makes me feel b-better.'

Alice said, 'Huh!' and turned away again.

'I w-wanted to tell you something . . . Obi Wanker Nobby!'

'*What*?'

'Obi Wanker Nobby . . . it's what my nan said.'

'What's it supposed to mean?'

'Obi-W-Wan Kenobi.'

A snort came bursting out of Alice. 'It sounds rude!'

'It's l-l-like a curse.'

'Obi Wanker Nobby!'

I'd known she would find it funny.

'Is it really what your nan said?'

'Yeah! Really!'

'You didn't make it up?'

'No!'

'You're not just saying it? To try and make me laugh?'

'I d-did make you laugh!'

Alice scowled and said, 'I suppose my mum's been

having a go at you? Trying to make me say *sorry*. Well, I won't! 'Cos I'm not. So there!'

'Why didn't you t-tell her it was to k-keep Sarah out? Then maybe she'd have understood.'

'She understands,' muttered Alice. 'She just pretends not to.'

'I know it doesn't seem f-fair,' I said, 'but S-Sarah's not as b-bright as you are. Sh-she—'

'She's cunning,' said Alice. 'She knows how to get her own way. And she hates me! She told me so. First day I came here. She pinned me up against the wall and said, *I hate you, I hate you. I'll always hate you.*'

'And you hate her?' I said.

'Yes! I told you. She hates me and I hate her!'

'Is it because of n-not doing for one what they w-wouldn't do for the other? Like you not being allowed to t-try for the High School?'

'No.' Alice said it scornfully. 'She can't help that. That's not her fault. That's *them*.'

'So why do you hate her? Just because she hates you?'

'She *greases*,' said Alice. 'She *worms*. She's repulsive!'

I had to agree that Sarah's behaviour could be squirm-making, especially the way she made up to her dad. But as I pointed out to Alice, she was very immature.

'She's v-very young for her age.'

'Don't make excuses for her! And don't stick up for her! She *enjoys* it.'

'Enj-joys what?' I said; but Alice had turned sullen again and wouldn't say.

'I thought we were f-friends,' I said. 'I've t-told you things about me!'

'And I've told you things about me!'

Yes, I thought, but some of those things weren't true. Like all the stuff she'd told me about her mother. Her real mother. She'd said her mother had come from a posh family and that her dad was an artist and her mum's family hadn't approved and so her mum had had to give her up for adoption. But I knew that wasn't true. And if she'd told me lies about that, who knew what else she had told me lies about?

'I d-don't think you've told me everything,' I said.

'No,' said Alice, ' 'cos you wouldn't want to know! I'm not very nice. I'm not a nice person! Ask your nan . . . she'll tell you! Everybody hates me. They all think I'm evil!'

I tried to protest, but she cut over the top of me.

'They think I'm ungrateful! Well, *I* didn't ask to be adopted!'

'But it's got to be b-better than being in a home?' I said.

She turned on me, in a fury. 'What do you know about it? You don't know anything!'

'How can I,' I said, 'if you won't tell me?'

I'd told Alice all my emotional secrets. I'd told her about Dad being ashamed of me. I'd told her about having Tourette's, how people laughed at me. How it

129

embarrassed me. I'd told her about Charlotte. How scared I was. I'd even let her read my crappy poem! All Alice did was yell – and tell lies.

'I th-thought we were meant to be f-f-f-*friends*! S-s-s-some f-friend you are!'

I scrambled up out of the hole and went blundering back up the garden.

'If that's the way you feel,' shrieked Alice, 'we needn't *be* friends any more!'

10

I didn't look for Alice next day. It was Sunday, so I knew
she would have to go to church in the morning; and she
probably wouldn't want to see me anyway. Not after
yesterday. She probably wouldn't ever want to talk to me
again.

'How about you coming with me, just for once?' said
Nan. 'Just to see what it's like . . . and to say thank you,
maybe.'

I frowned. 'Thank you for what?' I said.

'Thank you for Charlotte coming through the
operation,' said Nan.

I knew what Alice would say. Alice would say, what
kind of God was it who allowed Charlotte to get ill in the
first place? That was what Alice would say.

I tried saying it to Nan (but keeping Alice out of it).
Nan said, 'The way I see it, we're not puppets. We're
here on this earth to manage the best we can, it's up to
us how we do it. God's just up there keeping a watch
over us. He's not responsible for all the bad things that
happen.'

I wondered, in that case, why she should think he was

131

responsible for the good things. It seemed to me he either had to be responsible for both, or for neither. I didn't want to offend Nan, but Alice had got me interested in these things. I reckoned it was a fair question – if I could just manage to get it out.

Nan waited patiently through my splutterings and stutters. I've got to hand it to her, she took it on the chin. Not that she really had any answer.

'Ah, well, now,' she said, 'that's another matter. I happen to believe in the power of prayer. But if you want a really deep discussion, you should go to Norman. He's the one who's got the answers. All I'm saying is, why not come along and see for yourself?'

I was torn; I have to admit it. I had a kind of curiosity about what went on. Also about seeing Big Norm. On the other hand, Alice would be there; I wouldn't want her to think I was spying on her. It did have a sort of . . . *touristy* feel about it.

I muttered, 'M-maybe another time,' and Nan didn't push.

After she'd gone I went upstairs to the computer. Usually, for me, it's like pressing a magic button: the world and all its problems just disappear. I'm lost out there, in cyberspace! Today, it didn't happen. Thoughts of Alice kept intruding. I wished I hadn't lost my temper and yelled at her. She was so bright and sparky and funny, but she obviously wasn't happy. Something was seriously wrong, and if I was her friend I ought to be helping her, not bawling her out.

'Was Alice there?' I said to Nan, when she got back.

'Oh, yes, she was there,' said Nan, 'looking like a thundercloud. Little madam!'

After lunch, Nan said she thought we ought to go to the craft fair that was being held at the Fairfield Halls, in Croydon.

'I like a craft fair,' she said. 'You can pick up some really nice Christmas presents.'

When we arrived back there was an envelope on the mat. It had my name on it, and STRICTLY PRIVATE & PERSONAL in big capital letters. It was from Alice. Inside were more chapters of her story, with a note that said, 'You can read this if you like, but if you don't want to it doesn't matter.'

'What's that you've got?' said Nan.

'Just s-something Alice has done.'

'Strictly private and personal ... hm! More rude words, I suppose?'

Greatly daring, but feeling a sudden fierce loyalty towards Alice, I said, 'It's not v-very Christian to k-keep on ab-bout Alice like that.'

The minute I'd said it I thought that I shouldn't have done so, but Nan's really good at not taking offence. She's always very fair.

'You're right,' she said. 'It isn't Christian. Norman doesn't do it, and heaven knows he has enough to put up with.'

'It's not easy for Alice, either,' I muttered.

'I'm sure I don't know why!' said Nan. 'Nobody could be more loving than Norman. But I accept your criticism. I'll try to do better in future.'

While Nan sat down with the Sunday paper, I read my way through the next two chapters of Alice's story. When I had read them once, I went back and very carefully read them again. They were . . . weird. To say the least.

VI

Oh, what a dear little cottage! thought Alice. And what a sweet little baby!

She said the last bit out loud. She didn't altogether know where she was, but the Mock Purple and his friend the Purpose had quite disappeared, and so had Brighton beach. Now she seemed to be in someone's kitchen, with pots and pans all around. In one corner sat the Duchess (the same one who had hit her over the head with a soup ladle). The Duchess had a baby in her arms. Alice liked babies.

She ran over, eagerly, to look at it, only to find that it wasn't a baby at all, but a warthog. Alice reeled backwards and stepped straight on to the toes of the White Queen (who hadn't been there just a second before).

'Ouch!' screamed the White Queen. 'What a clumsy creature you are!'

'I do beg your pardon,' stammered Alice. Now, she thought, I shall get the blame for the fact that she has dropped all her stitches again.

The Duchess slung the warthog over her shoulder and rubbed its back. The warthog gave a loud belch.

'It needs a lullaby,' said the Duchess. 'You! Child!'

'Me?' said Alice.

'Well, you are the only child here, are you not? Sing us a lullaby, if you please.'

'I am not sure that I know any,' said Alice.

'Then invent one! You can do that, can't you?'

'I could try,' said Alice.

'Then try!'

Alice thought for a moment.

'Lullaby,' she said.

> 'Hush-a-bye, baby,
> Sleep safe in your bed.
> Roses are white,
> Prickles are red.
>
> Close the door firmly,
> Put on the lock.
> Sleep safe to the tick
> Tock tick of the clock.'

Alice secretly thought this was rather a good lullaby, but it seemed to put the Duchess in a frightful rage.

'What utter nonsense!' screamed the Duchess. 'What kind of a lullaby is that?'

'And what kind of a child,' said the White Queen, fretfully, 'would turn the key in its lock?'

'A disturbed one,' snapped the Duchess.

Disturbed is right, thought Alice. If it turns the key in the *lock, it might stand a chance of NOT being disturbed. But she didn't say so for fear of having the soup ladle thrown at her again. (For the warthog had disappeared and the Duchess was now standing at the stove, stirring something in a pot.)*

'Roses are white, prickles are red . . . it makes no sense,' said the White Queen. 'Roses,' she said to Alice, 'come in all colours. I really do not know where you get this kind of rubbish from!'

'She'll have copied it from somewhere,' said the Duchess, stirring very fast and furiously.

'On the contrary, I made up every word!' cried Alice.

'So you say. But you are a notorious liar.'

'No one can believe a word she says.' The White Queen cast Alice a reproachful look. 'Little girls who cannot learn to be grateful,' she said, 'can always be sent back where they came from.'

'Just remember that in future,' said the Duchess. 'We'll have no more of your nonsense!'

VII

Alice was wandering in a dark wood. I am completely lost, she thought. There is no way out! I shall be trapped here for ever.

She must have said the words aloud, without realizing, for a voice suddenly spoke to her from the undergrowth.

'Gloom and doom, gloom and doom. Do get your act together, for goodness' sake! We are all sick and tired of your constant moaning.'

Alice spun round, but could see nothing.

'Who is there?' she cried. 'Who is speaking?'

'I am the voice of the monster. Tee hee!'

The Cheshire Cat sprang out of the bushes and sat down on the path to begin washing itself. It licked a paw and wiped it delicately over its whiskers.

'You again!' cried Alice.

The Cat leered.

'Had you fooled, didn't I?'

'Yes, you did!' Alice said it crossly. 'If that is your idea of a joke, I think it was in very poor taste! I am in enough trouble as it is.'

'You are in a great deal of trouble,' said the Cat. 'But it is entirely your own fault. If you won't co-operate, what do you expect?'

Alice bit her lip. 'I suppose,' she said, without very much hope, 'you couldn't tell me the way out, could you?'

'There is no way out. You have already said so yourself.' The Cat waved a paw. 'You must just make the best of things.'

'I try,' said Alice. 'I do try! But sometimes it seems there is no best to be made.'

'Well, that is a matter of opinion,' said the Cat. 'That is only what YOU think. It may not be what others think. Others may think it is time you learnt to be a little more grateful. And what happened to that poem you were going to recite? The one that was written in the English language?'

'Nothing happened to it,' said Alice. 'You disappeared before I could tell it to you.'

'Excuses,' said the Cat. 'Nothing but excuses! Just get on with it.'

'Very well,' said Alice. 'But you probably won't like it. Nobody seems to like anything I do. But I will give it a go.'

She cleared her throat.

' "You are old, dear Papa," said the child to the man,
And your hair will soon turn into grey.
Yet you get up to tricks whenever you can.
Don't you think you should call it a day?

"You claim to be holy," the poor child said.
You claim to be whiter than white.
Yet the sins you commit are the deepest of red.
Pray how can you say this is right?

"Y–" '

'Stop!' The Cat swished its tail, angrily. 'I have heard enough! That is not at all an appropriate poem for a young girl to recite.'

'I knew you wouldn't like it,' said Alice, sadly.

'Then why on earth did you inflict it on me? If you cannot think nice thoughts, it is better you do not think at all.'

'I have another one,' said Alice. Nobody could accuse her of not trying. 'Perhaps you may like this one a little better. Shall I say it?'

'If you must.' The Cat spread out a paw and inspected its claws. 'Well? What are you waiting for?'

'The Walrus and the Little Girl,' said Alice. 'This is how it goes . . .

'The Walrus and the little Girl
Went walking, just the two.
The Walrus wept like anything,
At what he planned to do.
"I cannot help myself," he said.
"I know it's hard on you.

"If all the saints," he said, "came down,
And wept for half a year,
They could not clean my sins away,
Nor make my conscience clear.
Forgive me all my trespasses!'
He cried, and shed a tear.

"Be kind, my child! Be generous!"
The Walrus did beseech.
And out he stretched with both his hands
And smiled and showed his teeth.
"Do not be harsh! I only ask
To walk along the beach."

"If that were all," the Child thought,
"It would not be so bad."
It seemed a shame to be unkind,
And make the Walrus sad.
But as she stepped out by his side,
He turned into her dad!

"Oh, how I weep for you!" he said.

"I know it is not right!
But pray be good and humour me,
And don't put up a fight."
And then the sun went in because
It was the middle of the night.'

After Alice had finished reciting, there was a long silence.

'So . . . what do you think?' said Alice, timidly.

'What, what?' The Cat woke up, with a start. 'Have you finished? Is it over?'

'You mean, you weren't listening?' cried Alice.

'I am not in the habit,' said the Cat, 'of listening to lies and unpleasantness. What an extremely nasty child you are! If I ever catch sight of you again, I shall take very good care to keep out of your way.'

And with that the Cat dived into the undergrowth and was gone. Alice was left by herself. No one likes me, she thought. No one cares. I believe I shall just have to give up.

'So, is it any good?' said Nan.

Slowly, I nodded.

'It certainly seems to be absorbing, whatever it is.'

'It's a story,' I said.

'About what?'

'About . . . a girl.'

'Oh, yes?'

Nan's tone was encouraging. I knew that she was trying to show an interest because of what I'd said earlier, about her attitude not being very Christian. I wished I could just pass the story over to her and let her read it for herself. See what her reaction was. Whether she took it seriously, or whether she would just dismiss it as fantasy. I was getting these really bad feelings. Alice had sworn me to secrecy, but the things she was writing were starting to frighten me. They were scary! They would still be scary even if she was just making them up. But was she? That was what I needed to know. Because how could you tell? How could you decide if such things were true, or only make-believe?

'So what happens?' said Nan. 'To this girl? I suppose she meets a gorgeous hunk and falls in love?'

I shook my head. 'It's a b-bit s-scary,' I said. 'I can't decide whether it's t-true or whether it's s-something she's m-made up.'

Nan clicked her tongue. 'She'll have taken it from somewhere.'

'Why does everyone always s-*say* that?'

Nan looked at me in surprise. 'Say what?'

'That she'll have taken it from somewhere! You all ac-cuse her of telling l-*lies*, then you say she c-*copies* things!'

'I'm only repeating what Norman says. He's her father. He ought to know.'

I put my thumb in my mouth and started chewing.

'Don't do that,' said Nan. 'You'll make yourself sore. What's the matter? What's upsetting you?'

I tore off a piece of skin. My thumb immediately started to bleed.

'Is it that?' Nan pointed an accusing finger at Alice's story. 'Is it something she's written? Because if that's the case—'

'N-nobody l-*listens*!' I said.

If I could only write, like Alice could write, I could invent another chapter for her. I could bring myself into the story. I could be an Oddball, wandering in the forest, and I could bump into Alice and tell her that I was on her side, that I would try to help her. I would lead her out of the dark wood.

But I can't write. I can spell OK, and I have quite a good vocabulary. But I don't have any imagination. I'm quite a prosaic sort of person.

On the other hand, I could always try typing out some ideas. I could leave it to Alice to work out the details. Then she could write it in her own words. And maybe together we could find a way out. Maybe at last she would talk to me, and tell me the truth. I couldn't do anything if she wouldn't talk to me!

'Where are you off to now?' said Nan.

'I'm just going up to use the computer,' I said. 'I won't be long.'

I could at least make some suggestions. It would be up to Alice whether she used them or not.

SUGGESTIONS FOR NEXT CHAPTER.
Alice bumps into an Oddball in the Dark
Wood. She tells him her story and he
listens. He believes her. The Oddball does

not think she is any of the things that people say she is.

Alice asks the Oddball what she should do, and the Oddball says he thinks that she should ring Childline.

End of Chapter.

Next Chapter.
Alice rings Childline and comes out of the Dark Wood.

I printed out the page and put it in an envelope, wrote PLEASE READ! STRICTLY PERSONAL AND PRIVATE on the front and slipped Alice's chapters in with it.

On my way down the hall I put my head round the sitting-room door. Nan was nodding in her chair, with the newspaper spread out on her lap.

'I'm just going round to Alice's,' I said. 'Just to give her her story back.'

'Round the front,' said Nan.

Obediently, I went round the front. It was Sarah who came to the door.

'I've got s-something for Alice,' I said.

'I'll give it to her,' said Sarah.

She held out her hand, but I didn't trust Sarah. Certainly not with Alice's story.

'Who's come knocking at *my* door?' Alice's dad had appeared. 'Why, 'tis the young master! And what can we do for you, kind sir?'

Sarah said, 'He's got something for Alice, but he won't let me have it.'

I felt my cheeks fire up. 'It's p-private!'

'Private, is it? Well, now, young man, we don't have any secrets in this house, you know! We're a family.'

Desperately, I said, 'But it's s-something I've written.'

'Oh! Well! In that case, I suppose we shall have to make an exception. We can't impose our rules on other people, can we? Not everyone thinks the same way we do. Sarah, go and fetch your sister. Tell her there's a young man with something for her . . . something private!'

I stood awkwardly in the hall. There was the banging of a door, footsteps along the landing, and Alice came charging down the stairs. She snatched the envelope from me and went charging back up without a word. Her dad's voice thundered after her: '*Alice! Have you forgotten your manners?*'

'Thank you!' yelled Alice.

Later that evening I was in the garden, idly kicking a ball about, when there was a hissing, and Alice's head bobbed over the wall.

'Hey! Oddball!'

I rushed over.

'Take this.' She pushed an envelope at me.

'What is it?'

'Just *take it*! I've got to go!'

Alice sped off. I opened the envelope she had given me. There was just the one page inside it, with a note: THIS IS THE LAST CHAPTER.

I settled down, with my back against the wall, to read it.

VIII

Alice was still lost in the dark wood. She seemed to be in the middle of a conversation, though how it had got started she was not at all sure.

'The fact is,' said Alice.

'Fact?' cried the Duchess. 'A fact from you would be a fine thing!'

'It is a fact,' said Alice. 'There are things that come at one. That is a fact.'

'Baaa,' bleated the White Sheep, shaking out her knitting. 'Slip one, slop one.'

'In the night,' said Alice. 'That is when they come.'

'Knit two together,' bleated the Queen. And to Alice she said, 'I don't want to know!'

'Nobody wants to know. It is all lies!' shrieked the Duchess. 'Children who cannot learn to be grateful can always be sent back where they came from. Just remember that and guard your tongue.'

'Off with it! Off with it!' The Red Queen came galloping past. In her hand she held a pair of scissors. 'Off with her tongue!'

'Silence her, silence her!'

'Children who TELL–'

'Deserve what they get!'

This is it, thought Alice. This is where it all finishes. This is . . .

THE END

The end of the story? It left me feeling even more disturbed than I had before. It left me feeling creepy. If it hadn't been for giving Alice my word I would have gone straight in and shown it to Nan. But I knew I couldn't do that; not without Alice's permission.

I made up my mind that tomorrow was the day when she was going to talk to me. Bad things were happening – things I didn't even want to think about. Someone had to help her; and who else was there, if not me?

11

Monday morning I was up and dressed before Nan had even finished her breakfast.

'What's all this?' she said. 'You're very keen, all of a sudden!'

'Got things to do,' I said.

'Oh?' Nan waited. 'Anything interesting?'

I made a mumbling sound and stuffed two pieces of bread in the toaster.

'Going to see that Alice, I suppose. No!' Nan checked herself. 'That's a bad habit. You're quite right; I must stop it.'

'I am going to s-see her,' I said.

'You're a funny boy!' Nan shook her head. 'Wouldn't you have more fun with Steven? Playing football?'

'Don't p-play football,' I said. I only play football when I have to. Like at school, where it's compulsory.

'Well, what about the machine?' said Nan. 'Steven's got one. You could go and play games on it, or whatever it is that you do.'

'I've got to see Alice,' I said.

'Oh, all right! Suit yourself. I don't want to dictate

your choice of friends. I don't quite know what you see in her, but—'

'She's f-funny,' I said. 'She makes me l-laugh.'

She treated me like a human being, instead of a freak. And right now, I had this feeling that she needed me. I said this to Nan.

'Needs you in what way?' said Nan.

'She's n-not happy,' I said.

'No; I would agree with that,' said Nan. 'She's not a happy child. In spite of everything Norman's done for her.'

'S-something's n-not right!'

Nan sighed. 'I'm afraid it's Alice herself who's not right. She has a very violent nature. She's not an easy child to love. But, Duffy, you have enough to cope with! You can't shoulder her burdens as well. Alice must find her own salvation. If only she would just . . . *give* a little. Norman has so much love to offer her!'

I muttered, 'Maybe that's p-part of the p-problem.'

'Now, look,' said Nan. 'I know some people find him a bit . . . overwhelming. I know there are some, even in our congregation, who complain that he – well, that he has a tendency to take over. He can't help it! He gets enthusiastic, he gets carried away. He's got a big personality. Some people can't cope, it makes them feel threatened. But there's no need! He's a good man. Who else would have taken on a child like Alice? If she would just go halfway to meet him! It would make him so happy. And then she would be happier, too. Why does she have to fight him all the time?'

I had no answer to that. Or if I had, it was one I wasn't yet ready to face.

'Listen, I have to be off,' said Nan. 'I'll see you at lunchtime. And don't worry about Alice! There's nothing you can do, and anyway, she's in safe hands. Norman's the expert. I mean, it's his job! What do you and I know?'

Nothing, I thought, glumly. Or perhaps we didn't want to?

The minute Nan had gone, I crammed the last bit of toast into my mouth, snatched up the envelope containing Alice's final chapter and went racing down the garden. Alice wasn't there. *Damn.* That meant going round the front and seeing Sarah, and Granny Gregory. But it had to be done. I had to talk to her! That last chapter she had written had given me really bad feelings. It was like a cry for help, and I was the only one who seemed to be listening.

It was Sarah, again, who came to the door.

'Oh, it's you,' she said.

I started to ask if I could see Alice, but before I could get any words out the sound of a voice raised in anger came thudding up the hall. It was Alice's dad.

'If you think this is punishing us, you're quite mistaken! You're only punishing yourself!'

'Your d-dad's home,' I said. I hadn't bargained on that.

'Yes,' Sarah simpered. 'He's late for work. It's her fault. She's stopped talking.'

'S-stopped t-talking?' I said.

149

'She hasn't said a single word since five o'clock yesterday.' Sarah announced it with relish. She giggled. 'She's lost her tongue!'

I was getting that bad feeling again. Big splatty goose feet went plopping all up and down my spine. Alice's mum came out of the kitchen.

'Oh! Duffy,' she said. 'I'm sorry, this isn't an awfully good time.'

'I'll try again l-later!' I said.

I rushed back round the block, let myself into the garden and went racing down to sit on the wall. Sooner or later, Alice would come out. Her mum and dad would go off to work, and she would come looking for me. I had to be there, ready.

While I was waiting, I saw the fox come back to her earth. I saw her, she saw me. We both immediately froze. I sat there, scarcely daring to breathe. What was she doing out, at this time of day? She should have been home hours ago! I willed her to move, and at last she did, slinking low to the ground, one eye still fixed on me. I heaved a sigh of relief as she finally disappeared into the undergrowth. Safe! Now I just wanted Alice to come, so that I could tell her about it.

I had a long time to wait. It was another half an hour before Alice appeared. My backside was starting to grow numb, from sitting all that while on the wall.

'Alice!'

She came towards me, but she wasn't looking at me. I wasn't even sure that she had seen me. Sarah, with a kitten in her arms, came prancing after.

'It's no use talking to her,' she said. 'She won't say anything.' She held out the kitten, pushing it at Alice. 'Cat's got your tongue, cat's got your tongue!'

'Stop that,' I said.

Sarah's head jerked round in surprise.

'S-stop tormenting her!'

'Do what I like!' said Sarah. She stuck out her tongue. 'None of your business! Nothing to do with you. *She* can't do this.' She waggled her tongue in Alice's face. 'She's lost hers!'

'What a p-perfectly horrible b-brat you are,' I said.

'You can't talk to me like that!' shrilled Sarah. 'I'll tell my dad of you!'

'T-tell him what you like.'

'I will!' shrieked Sarah. 'I'll tell him!'

'Sarah!' Granny Gregory was coming down the garden. 'Stop it! Get back indoors. And you!' She turned on me. 'Take that girl and get her out of my sight before I do something I shall regret.' She grabbed Alice by the shoulders and yanked her towards the wall. 'Get yourself over there! And stay over there. You're not wanted here. Talk about ingratitude! You're breaking that man's heart. He tries so hard. So hard! And this is how you repay him. You little . . . *monster*! Just get her out of my sight! And don't bring her back until she's learnt some manners, or I shan't answer for the consequences.'

I jumped down into my own side of the garden. Alice, pushed by her grandmother, came toppling after. Quite calmly, she picked herself up. I was the one who was trembling.

'Let's g-go for a w-walk,' I said.

Alice didn't say anything. She followed me back down the garden, out through the side gate and into the road.

'W-where shall we go?' I said. 'Shall we go to the p-park?'

Alice shrugged. I took it as meaning that she wasn't bothered where we went, so I set off in the direction of the little park where last year, at about this same time, I'd walked with Mum and Nan, and Charlotte in her buggy.

'S-saw the fox just now,' I said. I told Alice how I'd watched her, watching me; how at last she had plucked up courage and made a run for her earth.

'Think there've been f-fox cubs,' I said. Nan had complained – though she obviously hadn't really minded – how they had romped about the garden, all among the flowerbeds, making mayhem.

Alice still said nothing. We walked for a long time in silence.

'Read your l-last chapter,' I said, after we'd been all round the park once and were on our second circuit. 'Look, I've got it here.' I handed her the envelope. 'Did you r-read my n-notes?'

Alice hunched a shoulder. I couldn't decide whether that meant she had or she hadn't. It could mean that she had – and hadn't found them useful. Or it could simply mean that she hadn't bothered. It was really very difficult to hold a conversation with someone who wouldn't talk.

'I know the R-Red Queen said c-cut off your t-tongue,' I said. 'But that was only in the story! You can still t-talk to *me*.'

But she wouldn't. Or couldn't. I wasn't sure which. In the end, in desperation, I said, 'We're going to have to go back, now. It's l-lunchtime.' It was gone lunchtime; it was nearly two o'clock. Nan would be wondering where I was.

Alice turned, unprotesting, and silently accompanied me back up the road. Even though it was late, and I knew that Nan would be going spare, I took her to her own front door and waited till someone came. I was scared if I left her she might just go on wandering.

It was Granny Gregory, this time, who opened the door. Sarah stood behind her.

'Oh,' said Granny Gregory. She sniffed. 'So you've come back, have you? That's a pity! I was hoping we might be rid of you.'

Alice, without a word, walked straight past and up the stairs.

'We've had a really good time without you!' shrilled Sarah. 'I said maybe you'd got run over.' She cackled. 'Needn't think I'd have cared!'

It really shocked me, her talking like that. What shocked me even more was the old woman, not saying anything. Sarah was immature, she couldn't help it. But surely her grandmother ought to stop her? The old girl just stood there, letting her spew it all out.

'I'd *like* it if she got run over! I'd like it if I never had to see her again!'

153

'She oughtn't to s-say things like that!' I said.

'Oh, really?' said Granny Gregory. 'And what do you know about it? You know nothing! You have no idea. You don't know what we've had to put up with. Lies, tantrums, bad temper . . . I'll thank you,' she said, 'to just keep your nose out of other people's business, young man!'

The door slammed in my face. Considerably shaken, I turned and walked back to Nan's. I'd thought it was bad in the old days, when Mum and Dad had had their rows, and Dad had made Mum cry; but nothing that either Mum or Dad had said, not even when they were both shouting at the tops of their voices and hurling accusations, had been as bad as the things Granny Gregory and Sarah had said about Alice.

Nan, as I'd known she would be, was in a state. She pounced on me the minute I came through the door.

'Where have you been? I've been worried half out of my mind! I rang old Mrs Gregory and she said you'd gone off somewhere with Alice. What time of day do you call this? I was expecting you back for lunch! I don't mind you going out,' said Nan, 'so long as you let me know where you are. You've got a mobile; why didn't you take it with you? And where exactly have you been, anyway?'

'Just w-walking,' I said.

'Just walking. And me sitting here imagining heaven knows what! Now I suppose you'll want something to eat?'

She didn't let up once, all the time that I was eating. I didn't try to defend myself; I felt guilty about worrying her. Nan had been good to me and Mum. She had offered us a home with her, if ever we wanted it (but we had to stand on our own feet, was what Mum said); she had taken me for the whole of the summer, and done her best to entertain me and keep my spirits up. It wasn't fair to take advantage. But then she started on Alice, and that wasn't fair, either.

'I hear she's been upsetting everyone, especially her poor father. I'm not being un-Christian! I'm just stating a fact. In some kind of monumental sulk, I gather. Won't communicate. What's brought this on? I suppose she didn't tell you? Poor Mrs Gregory! The old lady, I mean. Almost beside herself. She has to bear the brunt, you know. During the holidays. Many's the time she's had to separate those two girls before Alice could do some kind of mischief. Well! I *say* mischief. More like assault and battery. She'll do some serious damage one of these days. Now what's the problem? What's with all the movement?'

I'd gone into overdrive. Into munching mode. I opened my mouth and my arm shot out, narrowly missing the milk jug.

'I th-th-th—'

'All right, just calm down,' said Nan. 'Take it slowly. Let it come.'

'I th-th—'

I flailed, desperately. It's what happens when I get wound up. It's like I'm a puppet and some mad puppet master's jerking all my strings.

'Take a deep breath, there's no rush. We've got all day.'

Nan removed the milk jug, and my glass. 'Now! Try again.'

'I th-th-th—' It wasn't any use. The words had got jammed. I sprang up and made for the door, beckoning Nan to follow.

'What's this?' said Nan. 'Where are we going?'

'Up!'

'Not that blessed machine?' said Nan.

'Yes!'

I led the way into the computer room. I sat down at the console and pulled up a chair for Nan. Sometimes it was easier to write things than to say them. Like Alice, with her story.

'Go on, then!' said Nan. 'You've got my attention. What's it all about?'

I began tapping out the words. I think something terrible is happening to Alice.

'Like what?' said Nan.

Like the red queen has cut out her tongue and she can't talk.

'You mean she's in a sulk.'

It's not a sulk. I think it's her dad.

'What?' Nan looked at me, instantly alert. 'What do you mean, her dad? What are you trying to say?'

I knew Nan wasn't going to accept it. I knew she was going to blow up. But I had to try!

I think her dad is doing things to her.

Nan's lips had gone very tight. 'What kind of things?'

Bad things. Like touching her.

'Did that child tell you this?'

Even if she had, Nan still wouldn't believe it.

She didn't exactly tell me, I typed.

'Then why are you even hinting at it?'

I wished I had Alice's gift of language. Without the right words, how could I ever hope to convince Nan of what to her was the unthinkable? It had been unthinkable to me until I'd read those last two chapters. I was Alice's friend, and even I had been reluctant to believe her.

'*Well?* I'm waiting!' said Nan.

'I'm s-scared for her,' I said. 'I'm really s-scared!'

'Why? Give me some facts! Something to go on.'

'I c-can't,' I said. 'I p-promised her I w-wouldn't s-say anything!'

'Then it's better you don't!' Nan's whole body was stiff with outrage. 'That man is practically a saint in my book. I won't hear a word against him! If it hadn't been for him, I would never have survived when your granddad died. I can't tell you what a comfort he was! Your mum was too bound up with Charlotte, it wasn't her fault. But I was feeling very down, and it was Norman saw me through it. And I'm not the only one! You ask anybody in our church. They'll tell you! He's very highly respected in this community. He did a magnificent thing, adopting those two, and I won't have him brought low by a poison-tongued little girl! Now, switch that thing off and stop all this nonsense. I told you right at the beginning, didn't I? I warned you. That child lives in a fantasy world. The lies just pour out of her. She probably doesn't even realize that they are lies, that's what makes her so dangerous. I don't want you repeating to anyone else what you've said to me. Is that understood?'

I nodded.

'So long as it is! I'm not having that man put under any extra strain. He's got enough on his plate. This is the sort of thing,' said Nan, in disgusted tones, 'that you read about in the tabloids.'

Did that make it not true? Was Alice's story really just a fantasy, as Nan claimed? The product of a damaged mind? Or was she writing about things that were actually happening? She'd lied to me about her mother, and that was a pretty big sort of lie. But maybe if you'd been adopted and you weren't happy and everybody seemed to be against you, you would feel the need to make up lies; to invent a new past for yourself. I could understand that.

I thought of Alice's dad. Big Norm; pillar of the community. All hale and hearty and outgoing, with his jokes and his funny voices and his flaming hair and beard. I'd thought how great it would be to have a dad like that! I'd agreed with Nan that Alice ought to show a bit more gratitude.

And then I thought of the Red Queen, in Alice's story. *Off-with her knickers!* And I'd laughed, thinking it was meant to be funny. But it wasn't.

That night when I went to bed, I couldn't sleep. Every time I closed my eyes I had visions of Red Queens and walruses, and bleating sheep and Duchesses. Lines from Alice's poems kept haunting through my head.

Beware the slippy slobbering, the gobble and the guzzle . . .
Close the door firmly, put on the lock . . .
But as she stepped out by his side, he turned into her dad . . .

In the end I couldn't stand it any more. I got out of bed and went over to the window, hoping that perhaps I might see the fox and her cubs. Anything to take my mind off Alice. To remove the burden of having to decide whether to do something – and if so, what – or whether to simply write her off as some kind of sick fantasist, which was what Nan would have me believe.

I didn't want to think of Alice as sick! But I didn't want to think of the other thing, either. If I thought of the other thing, then how could I just sit back and let it go on happening?

I stared out, ferociously, into the night. *The moral of this story reads, that no one cares for children's needs.* I swallowed – and at that moment, I saw Alice. A small white ghost flitting in the moonlight, on the other side of the wall. I guessed at once where she was headed: down the rabbit hole. She was going to disappear into her time warp, where she couldn't be got at.

It was one of those moments when you know without any question what you've got to do. You don't stand there hesitating, you just go ahead and do it. I snatched up my dressing gown, tiptoed out of my bedroom and trod as quietly as I could down the stairs. The bolts on the kitchen door were stiff. They made a horrible grinding noise as I pulled them back. I didn't wait to find out whether Nan had woken up, I shot straight out and down the garden.

'Alice?' I hoisted myself over the wall. I could see the white of her nightdress. She was crouched at the mouth of the hole, arms wrapped tightly round her knees, knees drawn up to her chin.

'Alice!' I crawled in next to her. 'Please s-speak to me! I want to help you. I'm not like all the others. I know what you're s-saying is t-true!'

She turned, very slowly, to look at me; searching my face as if to discover whether I really did believe her or whether I was just saying it. Until that moment, I hadn't actually been sure. Now, suddenly, I was.

Urgently, I whispered at her. 'S-suppose you did what the Oddb-ball suggested?'

A shudder ran through her. 'I can't!'

'W-why not?'

In a harsh shriek Alice cried out, 'Little girls who *tell*—'

'What?' I said. 'What?'

Her voice changed and became all soft and bleaty. 'I don't want to know, I don't want to know!'

'But s-someone has to know,' I said.

Alice's hands began frantically knitting. 'Slip one, slop one, now see what you've made me do! I've dropped all my stitches!'

'You can always p-pick them up again,' I said.

'No! No! Once they're gone, they're gone!' She looked at me, eyes wide with terror. 'You're ruining everything! You're ruining my entire life!'

'M-me?' I said.

'Not you!' Alice shook her head, vigorously. '*Her.* That girl. That Alice! What shall I do?' She began to rock, piteously, to and fro. 'What shall I do if she tells?'

I wondered who Alice was talking about. Who was she being when she was the White Queen? Was it her mum? I remembered how she had once questioned me about my mum. She had wanted to know how Mum had managed after Dad had left. She had said that her mum would never survive. Was she scared of telling because of what it might do to her mum?

This wasn't right!

'Alice,' I said, 'your mum will be OK! She's a grown-up. She'll manage. You've got to th-think of you!'

'Think of me, think of me . . .' She had the front of her nightdress scrunched between her hands and was twisting at it, wringing it out. '*How can you be so ungrateful?*'

'It's not being ungrateful,' I said. 'It's d-doing what has to be d-done. You can't go on like this! There has to be someone you can tell.'

She looked at me. 'Who?' she whispered. 'Who could I tell?'

All I could think of was Childline, but before I could get the word out I heard the scuffling of undergrowth on the other side of the wall. I thought it was the fox, but then I heard Nan's voice.

'Duffy! Are you there?' I crawled out of the hole and saw Nan's head silhouetted in the moonlight.

'I'm with Alice,' I said.

'Come back to the house,' said Nan. 'Both of you.'

I scrambled to my feet. Alice stayed where she was, curled into a ball.

'Come along!' said Nan. 'Bring Alice with you.'

I bent down. 'Alice?' I said; but she just curled up tighter and wouldn't move.

'Alice! Do what you're told,' said Nan. 'You can't stay out here. Come back to the house with Duffy.'

I held out my hand. Meekly, she took it. I led her to the wall and waited while she hauled herself over and slithered down the other side. She didn't do it with her usual spring and bounce, but almost in slow motion, as if she were in a trance, or sleepwalking.

Together, we followed Nan back to the house.

'Well, now,' said Nan. 'Let's all sit down and have a cup of tea – Duffy! Put the kettle on. Then we'll talk.'

'No one will listen!' I said.

'I'll listen,' said Nan.

She told me afterwards that just like me she hadn't been able to sleep for all the thoughts that were milling round her brain. She'd been 'looking back', she said. Turning over in her mind our conversation earlier in the day. There were things, she said, which had bothered her. She didn't say which things; not at the time. It was only later she admitted that she had occasionally been disturbed by the way Sarah had behaved around her dad, clutching and clinging in a manner, Nan said, that had never seemed quite right.

'I just closed my eyes to it . . . you don't like to think of things like that.'

That night, in the kitchen, she sat Alice down at the table, while I made the tea, and invited her to talk.

'Come on, Alice! I'm here – I'm listening. Tell me what's upsetting you.'

But Alice wouldn't; or maybe she simply couldn't. It was like the Red Queen had put a curse on her and struck her dumb. Nan tried coaxing and cajoling, but Alice just sat there, in silence.

'How about if it was just you and me?' said Nan. 'On our own?'

I didn't want to leave, but I would have done, if it would have made it easier for Alice. I could see she might not want me there, even though I was her friend. I could see it might be embarrassing. But Alice shook her head, quite violently, at Nan's suggestion.

'So what are we to do?' said Nan. 'Is there nobody at all you feel that you could talk to?'

'Alice!' I had a sudden idea. 'Why don't you let Nan read your story? Like I did?'

I could see that she was hesitating. I think she'd reached that stage of desperation where she knew, if she didn't let someone help her, she would be lost in the dark wood for ever.

'Shall I go and get it?' I sprang up, pushing my chair back. 'Is it down the hole? Shall I get it? I won't if you don't want me to! Just say.'

There was this long, tense pause; then very slowly she

nodded. I shot off up the garden, over the wall, and down into the undergrowth. I should have taken a torch, but the moon was almost full and in any case I quickly felt what I was looking for as I scrabbled around at the entrance to the hole: Alice's story, all wrapped up in plastic bags.

We went through to the sitting room, and Alice and I huddled together on the sofa while Nan unrolled the pages and read through them. She didn't say anything, and it was impossible to tell, from watching her face, what she was thinking. I was scared in case she might just dismiss them as fantasy. If she'd have done that, I would have felt that I'd let Alice down. That I'd failed her.

Nan came to the last page, and I waited, with my heart hammering, for what she would say. And then the telephone rang, and Nan picked up the receiver, and it was Alice's dad. I would have guessed who it was even if I hadn't heard his voice, booming out over the phone. To begin with, he boomed because that was his normal way of talking. He wanted to know if by any chance Alice was with us. Nan said that she was.

'I'll come round and get her.'

We both heard him say it; Alice and me. Alice didn't move, but a tremor ran through her. And then Nan said, 'I really think it would be best if she stayed here for the night.' She said it kind of apologetically – after all, this was Big Norm she was talking to – but she said it pretty firmly at the same time. That was when Alice's dad started booming in real earnest. He was coming round *straight away*. He demanded that Alice went back with him. Nan had no right to keep her there against his wishes.

Nan stuck to her guns; I've got to hand it to her. She stayed really calm and dignified. She told him to wait while she asked Alice what *she* wanted.

'Do you want to go with your dad?' she said. 'Or would you rather stay here?'

'Stay here,' whispered Alice; so Nan went back to the phone and said she was sorry, but she couldn't force Alice to do what she didn't want to do.

'I think it'd be best,' she said, 'if we sort things out in the morning. We'll all be a lot calmer. Alice is a bit upset just at the moment, and I expect you are, too, so—'

The phone was slammed down even as Nan was talking.

'Now is *not* the time for reasoned discussion,' said Nan. 'Don't worry,' she told Alice. 'You're quite safe here. I'll go and make up a bed in the spare room, and in the morning we'll do whatever has to be done.'

It was such a relief to have Nan on our side! I knew it must have been a really hard decision for her, worshipping Big Norm like she did. I never would have thought she'd be capable of standing up to him, which just shows how wrong you can be about people. I've always looked on Nan as – well! Quite soft and fluffy, if I'm to be honest. But she'd talked really tough on that telephone.

Nan was still upstairs making the bed when we heard the sound of a car pull up outside. There was a roar, and a great squeal of brakes. Alice immediately began to shake. I hated to see her like that! She'd always seemed so ready to take on the entire world. I hated that anyone could do this to her. I squeezed her arm.

'It's all right, they can't force you!'

I went over to the window in time to see Alice's mum push open the front gate.

'It's your mum,' I said. 'I think your dad's there as well, but he's staying in the car.'

He probably knew that Nan wouldn't let him in. I didn't think she would. She let Alice's mum in, though. The White Queen. I sat protectively on the sofa, next to Alice. She'd seen me through the worst of my fears about Charlotte; now it was up to me to do what I could for her.

'Alice!' Her mum said it sharply. 'Get up and stop being silly! I've come to take you home.'

Alice shrank back into the sofa. 'I can't! I can't ever come home!'

'What do you mean, you can't ever come home? Why can't you?'

'Because I've told them,' whispered Alice.

I know it sounds stupid, but I almost expected her mum to turn into the White Sheep, right there and then, and start knitting.

'You told them . . . what?' she said.

'About Dad,' whispered Alice. 'The things that he does to us . . . I'm sorry! I'm sorry!' The tears went chasing down her cheeks. There was something horribly disturbing about seeing Alice cry. 'I know I shouldn't have, but I couldn't help it! I had to tell someone, Mum! Please don't hate me!'

There was this long, long silence.

'Nobody hates you,' said Alice's mum. 'Stay here tonight. We'll . . . talk in the morning.'

So Alice stayed the night, and in the morning they all got together and talked, only I wasn't there. I'd done what I could, and now the grown-ups had taken over. I was excluded, as young people always are. I asked Nan, later, what was likely to happen. She said, 'It's in the hands of the social services. It's up to them.'

'But what will happen to Alice?' I said.

'She's being taken care of,' said Nan. 'She'll be all right now.'

'She won't have to go back where she came from, will she? She'd hate that! It wouldn't be fair!'

Nan hesitated. 'I can't answer that one,' she said. 'She'll maybe have to go into care for a little while. Just until they've . . . sorted things out.'

'Then what?'

'Well! Maybe then she'll be able to go back home.'

'What about . . . her dad?'

Nan's lips tightened. 'If they decide she's telling the truth—'

'She is!' I said. 'Nan, she is!'

'Yes. Well. In that case, I suppose . . .'

Nan's voice trailed off. She shook her head, helplessly. I knew it was difficult for her; she'd idolized Big Norm.

Even now she was finding it hard to admit he might be capable of doing anything wrong. I could understand that. He'd helped her a lot when Granddad had died. He was warm and funny and had made me laugh. But he'd adopted two girls who'd already had a rough start in life – Sarah, who needed special care and attention; Alice, who'd never had a home before – and he'd used them and abused them and set them against each other. The way I saw it, it didn't matter how good he'd been to Nan, he'd betrayed both Alice and Sarah.

All Nan could say was, 'People's behaviour isn't always easy to explain.' She said that Alice's dad was a 'deeply flawed personality'. For the moment, it was as far as she was prepared to go, and I didn't push her. I just felt grateful that in the end she'd listened.

I hung around in the garden a lot for the rest of that day, in the hopes of Alice coming out. I was just about to give up, when at last she appeared. She came running down to the wall, breathless and in a hurry.

'Oddball! They wanted me to go without saying goodbye to you.'

'Go where?' I said.

'They're taking us away. But it won't be for ever!'

'Will you be all right?' I said.

'Yes.' She nodded. 'I'll be all right.'

'You had to do it,' I said. 'Alice, you had to!'

'I know. Don't worry, Oddball! It'll all work out.' She brushed the back of her hand across her eyes. 'I hope Charlotte's OK. I really do! I'll be thinking about you.'

'M-me, too,' I said.

'Bye, then, Oddball!' Alice sprang up at the wall, dashed a quick kiss on my cheek and was off again, down the garden. 'I'll be in touch! I promise!'

That was a while ago. I've asked Nan once or twice if she knows what's happened, but she doesn't. She says that the old lady, old Granny Gregory, has gone into sheltered accommodation and that the house has been sold and Alice's mum has moved away. But she doesn't know where Alice is.

I wish she'd write to me! I have so many things I want to tell her. I want to tell her how I'm home again with Mum and Charlotte. How Charlotte's doing really well and Mum's been able to go back to work. How my poem that I wrote, my *Poem for Charlotte*, was published in the school magazine. We all had to write on 'a subject close to your heart', so I sent in my Charlotte poem, which was something I'd never dared to do before meeting Alice. I'd have been too scared of being laughed at. Maybe some people did laugh, but I don't care! Not any more. Not thanks to Alice.

Something else I want to tell her, I want to tell her how the school play last term was a musical of *Alice in Wonderland* and I volunteered to help backstage. The first time in my life I've ever taken part in an after-school activity! Plus I was the only person in my entire class who'd actually read the book. Mr Chinn (he was the producer) was well impressed! I reckon Alice would be, too.

I'm making a note of all the things I'm going to tell her when she writes to me. She *will* write; sooner or later. She promised that she would, and Alice is the sort of person who always does what she says she'll do.

She knows how to get in touch with me: she had Nan's address. One of these days I'll hear from her! And when I do, what I want to say more than anything else is a big THANK YOU. Thank you, Alice, for being there!